Eggpl

Boo.

3 Ménage Romances

Eggplant Canyon

Books 4-6

3 Ménage Romances

Sylvie Haas

Eggplant Canyon: Books 4-6 by Sylvie Haas

Cover Design: Bookin' It Designs

Ebook ISBN: 978-1-950166-62-6

Paperback ISBN: 978-1-950166-63-3

Table of Contents

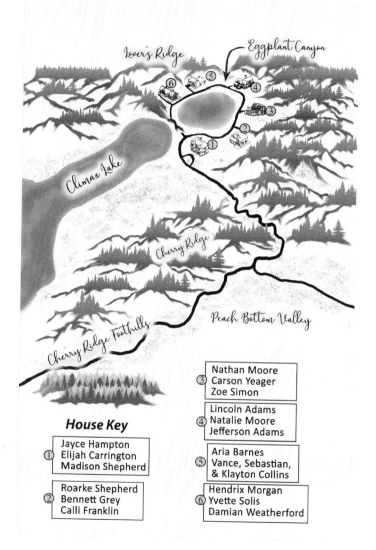

Lover's Ridge

Eggplant Canyon

Climax Lake

Cherry Ridge

Peach Bottom Valley

Cherry Ridge Foothills

③ Nathan Moore
Carson Yeager
Zoe Simon

④ Lincoln Adams
Natalie Moore
Jefferson Adams

⑤ Aria Barnes
Vance, Sebastian,
& Klayton Collins

⑥ Hendrix Morgan
Yvette Solis
Damian Weatherford

House Key

① Jayce Hampton
Elijah Carrington
Madison Shepherd

② Roarke Shepherd
Bennett Grey
Calli Franklin

Claimed by my Boss & His Twin

A Ménage Romance

Sylvie Haas

Blurb

Dropping papers off at my boss's house shouldn't be a big deal, except that I'm in love with him, and I have a little fantasy that he secretly feels the same.

Maybe that's why his sudden change in demeanor makes me think my fantasy is finally coming true.

It's not...and the second I realize my mistake, the storm of the century unleashes a mudslide, trapping me at his house.

It's way too late to question what could possibly go wrong. The only question remaining is if I'd rather save my job or my heart.

If you love dirty-talking men who have over-the-top ideas of how to please their woman and want to give her babies, these guys can double up your fantasy, too!

One

Natalie

Pulling into the driveway of my boss's luxurious mountain home in Eggplant Canyon, I hope my car doesn't drip oil on his pristine driveway. That's not the kind of mark I'd like to leave on his life. If I ever got to play out my fantasies, I'd leave lipstick on his collar, his chest, his co—I stop myself from imagining my boss's *eggplant*.

I give myself a mental shake and grab the large envelope with the contract he needs me to drop off. The errant thoughts will serve me just fine later, but for now, the most fun I can have is pretending I live with him and I'm coming home.

Be nice. Be pretty. Be useful. My mother's mantra plays through my mind. It may be a little ridiculous, but here I am, after hours, delivering a contract in between waves of the horrific storm.

Reaching under the chair, I feel around for the hidden key that he said is magnetically attached. When I don't find anything, I drop to my hands and knees to look. Still nothing.

Did I remember incorrectly? Checking the other chair and small table, there's no key. I poke around the porch at the edge of the bushes looking for a fake rock like my parents used to use.

He gave me one mission...leave the contract inside his house. I'd supposed my biggest problem would be refraining from testing how cozy his sofa is, or finding his bedroom and smelling his pillows—I'm not a creeper—but he probably has cameras and I'd end up fired.

But I can't even stick to my job and leave the contract inside if I can't find the key. I glance overhead at the sky full of black clouds. The small break in the storm isn't enough for me to trust leaving the contract on the porch.

Doing exactly what my boss asked would be ideal, but if I can't find the key, I suppose I can leave the contract at my brothers' house next door, then have one of them deliver it when Mister Adams gets home. Will I get points for thinking outside the box?

My boss and my brothers are friends. It was that connection that landed me the high-paying administrative assistant job that I can't afford to mess up.

I lose myself for a moment, staring at the ominous skyline cresting the mountain ridge opposite his house. It's a view I could get used to, but that will be from my siblings' house since our company has a strict 'no fraternizing' policy.

A chuckle bubbles through me...as if I'd have a chance to fraternize with my boss who barely ever looks my way.

The crack of the front door opening causes me to spin around. He's not supposed to get back in town until later. I spoke to him thirty minutes ago. Yet he's here.

My heart's beating out of control.

Is this more than a request for me to bring the contract? Am I ready for my fantasy world to be put to the test?

Wet heat pools between my legs in the brief second we stare at each other. He's so much more relaxed at home than at the office. His t-shirt hangs on him like it's an old favorite, there's no styling product in his hair, and his features are ever-so-slightly more relaxed... Like he's a different person.

Jefferson

Does my twin brother have a stalker?

The woman rustling around on his front porch causes me to think so. Lincoln's large glass windows give me an adequate view of the woman, although if she were to look, she wouldn't be able to see much of me with how the furniture is arranged.

Shifting from my relaxed sprawl on the couch, I sit forward with my hands on my knees, ready to go to the door. Even though she can't hear me, I suppress my groan when she gets on all fours.

Is it wrong to watch? Is it wrong for her to be snooping on my brother's porch?

I hesitate. What's wrong is that I want to pretend to be my twin and imagine having this gorgeous woman in my life.

Her business suit and bun, and the manilla envelope she's holding, give her an air of confidence like she belongs here. Why doesn't she knock?

I take that back. Looking under everything on the porch doesn't exactly scream that she belongs, but she's not looking over her shoulder or looking to see if he has one of those doorbell cameras.

Who is she? And what is she doing?

She rights herself, her hands and manilla folder flop to her sides, and she drops her head back. Is she looking at the sky?

Oh shit. I got in town a few days ago and haven't put Lincoln's hidden key back. As far as Lincoln knows, I'm supposed to be at a meeting with my lawyer, but he had to cancel, leaving me home unexpectedly.

I stride to the door and with every step I'm more curious who this woman is. She's gorgeous with a self-assured innocence. She's making my cock hard. She's exactly what I don't need right now.

I moved back to Eggplant Canyon and am working with a lawyer to get partial custody of my son, Harrison. My wild ways when I was younger cost me dearly. One of the few things I'd contributed to my son's life other than sperm, was that I'd asked my girlfriend to use a presidential name like my parents had done. Harrison is the one she chose. I appreciate that she extended that courtesy and did such a great job of raising him on her own up until this point.

It's ten years past when I should have gotten my shit together and shown that I could be stable.

So why the fuck is temptation on my brother's front porch? Why when I pop the door open do I feel an instant connection to the innocent beauty? Not the kind I'd had with hookups but the kind that tells me I have to get to know this woman. Why the hell am I imagining her belly swollen with my baby while she carries another on her hip?

"I have your contract." Her voice is soft and delicate, like her. She holds up the folder. A business associate? That explains the clothes, but she's too young. Her innocence could be deceiving, but I don't place her much above a teenager.

Her big eyes look up at me with more than a business relationship brewing behind them.

"Right," I say, opening the door further. This isn't right, but I can't find it in me to tell her who I am. Devilish thoughts play through my mind.

"I should go." She looks at me with hope and desire while extending the envelope. Her eyes rake down my t-shirt and athletic shorts, the same as most women do. Thankfully, I manage to keep my cock from tenting my pants.

All of the self-control I'd been so proud of lately is urging me to invite her in, which can't possibly work out. This is going to be wrong on a few levels.

"Wait." My words pull her eyes back to mine and the faintest hint of pink covers her cheeks before her expression turns to something akin to idolizing.

This insanely gorgeous woman idolizes my twin? Time to explore. Nothing will happen. He'll be home soon. He'll have to fess up that he has a carbon copy...physically anyway. His corporate path and my entrepreneurial struggles bear no resemblance.

"Come on in."

Her eyes go wide and she worries her lower lip. That does a number on my cock, but I remind it we're going to bed alone tonight.

"You want me to come in?" Why is she surprised? This rules her out as a girlfriend or mistress.

I test the waters. "Sure, why not."

She enters and glances around as if she's never been inside before. "What a beautiful home you have, Mister Adams."

That *is* my name, and this will be my home for the next few months. "Make yourself comfortable."

"I thought I was just dropping this off. I didn't plan to stay. You said to use the key—"

"I didn't expect to get in until later." The truth fits rather well, and old habits find my hand on her lower back as I guide her to the living room.

She glances down, where my arm disappears behind her, and from the angle her head is turned, I see a hint of a smile. Has my brother ever touched her like this? Does he see her for the doll that she is?

Welcoming her into my home feels so right, like my hand is where it belongs. Lincoln's may not belong there, but mine does. But old habits are exactly that...old...not me anymore. I promised myself not to date anyone until I got my son back.

The problem is that the tightness in my chest and the primal need to please her feel so *new*. This isn't how I pick up women. It was always in a bar with lots of alcohol and bad decisions. She hesitantly makes herself comfortable in a high-backed easy chair. I'm about to take the seat across the room when I remember my manners.

"Would you like something to drink?"

"Sparkling water would be great." She sets the contract on the table and pats it.

I return with our drinks, no better able to control my attraction to her. She studies my every move.

Lincoln and I had fun tricking people when we were younger. It was a rare chance to live in someone else's shoes. Let's call this a trip down memory lane.

"What's on your mind? You look curious."

She purses her lips, takes a sip, and looks everywhere but at me.

"Am I that scary to talk to?"

"You're so different at the office. You never..." She pauses then waves her hand between us. "Anyway, it's good to see that you're relaxed at home. Sometimes, at the office, I worry that you work too hard."

I can't stop myself? "Work hours are over. Let your hair down, and take your jacket off. Hang out...relax."

Her brow furrows.

"What do you have to lose?" This feels so right.

"I don't..." Her thoughts weigh heavily.

Would we both be put at ease if I simply told her I'm not my brother? I don't want her to get freaked out that I'm a stranger. She might leave, and I wouldn't be able to handle that. I have to be near her a few more minutes, then I'll come clean.

"Tell me about yourself. What do you do to relax?"

"Read books."

"Is that it?"

She shrugs. "Lots of books."

"Let your hair down."

Her hand flies to her chest. "Mister Adams..."

"Or I can do it for you." Fuck. I shouldn't have said that. It would be my preference to run my fingers through her silky strands, find the little clip that's holding her together, and undo her. That would be the old me. I'm on thin ice, but the flicker of excitement in her eyes lures me further.

Her blush takes over her entire cheeks. Angling her face to the side, away from me, she holds her bun with one hand and timidly retrieves two bobby pins. When she pulls her hands away, her hair spills down, signaling my cock to wake up. She rakes her fingers through her hair, each stroke a virtual brush over my thickening rod.

"There, now you look relaxed too. Doesn't that feel better?"

She ducks her head. Intending to refresh her drink, I head to her, but when I'm close and can see the subtleties of the golds and blondes in her rich brown hair, I lose focus.

I stroke a finger over her ear. "You're gorgeous."

Two

Natalie

"Thank you." Years of etiquette, of how a young woman is supposed to behave are ingrained in me so the pleasantry flows off my tongue easily. The shallow breaths, the lightheadedness, and the excitement over my fantasy coming true make it impossible to utter anything else.

Forcing breaths deeper into my lungs, I regain what composure I can. Mister Adams has switched from his normal expensive musky cologne to a new one that I can only describe as the perfect combination of spice and sex. It invades every pore, every thought, every bit of my being.

With my back straight, ankles crossed, and mangled bobby pins in my hands, I say, "You are very attractive too."

In my fantasies, I'm much more eloquent, and I also wouldn't still be making metal origami out of my hairpins. My plan, if that's what a fantasy could loosely be called, was to let my boss release all of my sexual frustrations with a single kiss.

Anything he did after that could be considered a Christmas bonus.

"Let me take those before somebody gets hurt." His large hand cups mine, doing so much more than removing my pins. He's owning me, protecting me, giving me a promise, and I don't even feel silly reading that much into it. He shoves the metal carnage into his pocket.

I'm so lost in my fantasy that I can't tell what's real anymore. While I roll around in my maybe-real, maybe-not bliss, he continues, "So you like the way I wear the casual look?" His voice is like melted butter on my popcorn.

"It's like you're a whole different person. There's the Mister Adams from the office and then there's…"

Accumulation of drool as I'm trying to speak causes me to cut myself off so I can swallow, and not just because I got myself thinking about buttery popcorn.

He stares at me, contemplating something. "I am—"

A low rumble rocks my world and for a split second, I think it's a reaction to my boss. I reflexively grasp the arms of my chair, but it's not until I note the concern on his face that I realize the rumble was real. I've never been in an earthquake, but I imagine it would feel like that.

I'm happy to stay put while he checks the house and looks out the windows. The chance to breathe is useful. Am I willing to see where this goes? Which lines will I let him cross? I fan myself as heat overtakes me at the thought of my boss being my first.

The swagger in his stride as he re-enters the room steals my breath all over again. "Everything's in place."

He stops beside my chair. When I angle my head up, looking at him from under my lashes, he says, "It must have just been my heart pounding when you let your hair down."

The sexual confidence oozing from him is the counterbalance to my sexual innocence. His finger tucks under my chin, breaching untouched territory. The things I'm feeling are so much stronger now that I have his attention. At work, I'm his robot secretary, or that's how it feels since he handles as much as possible through purely professional emails.

Has he been thinking of me too? Is there any way around the company's fraternization policy, because I think we're about to violate it? Not likely they'll grant a waiver just because my virginity's involved.

"What the fuck!" My boss's voice booms through the room a split second before the front door slams.

I may have just felt an earthquake, but there's a whirlwind in my brain as I glance from the sexy, relaxed version of my boss who's standing beside me to the uptight, angry version in the entry. If his shoes and the bottoms of his pants weren't covered in mud, I'd easily determine that the one in the entry is real.

Did my mind conjure the one beside me? I extend a finger from the arm of the chair to check. The heat of his body, the firmness of his thigh, and the jerk of his head downward in response to my touch indicate that he's far more than a figment of my imagination.

Three

Lincoln

"What the fuck!" My words come out louder and harsher than I'd intended, but they're accurate.

Jefferson said he'd changed his ways. He had a solid start on building a security company as part of his effort to settle down, yet
here he is with his hand on my girl. The problem is that nobody, including her, knows that she's my girl.

I let the mud on my shoes cement me to the floor in the entry because if I go near my brother, I'll be tempted to pummel him. The thought sends a shiver down my spine. I'm driven and competitive, but not violent.

He glances down at Natalie long enough that I'm left out of whatever's going on between them. I ball my fists then force my fingers to straighten. Back-to-back meetings in the city had been exhausting, not to mention my white-knuckle drive through the horrendous storm, but that was nothing compared to my car getting caught in a mudslide on the way home and having to walk the last bit, but that has nothing on seeing Jefferson touch Natalie. I don't even allow myself that luxury.

"Explain," I demand.

Natalie jumps up, smooths her skirt, and clasps her hands. "I can't."

It's the first time she's been stumped. No matter the situation that arises, she handles it with grace. She's the best damned administrative assistant I've had, and it just about kills me to leave it that way. I want her as so much more. I'd been breaking lately, my thoughts wandering to her more and more, even in the middle of the night. I shove all of that aside.

Jefferson steps between Natalie and me, holding his hands up. "Calm down, we were just talking."

"Get away from her."

He side-steps, and even though it's not as far as I'd like, I let it go.

"Miss Moore, I see you met my twin brother, Jefferson." I pause to gauge the look on her face—confusion that quickly shifts to surprise. That tempers how I continue. "Apparently he's not above our childish games of switching places."

"Calm the fuck down," Jefferson says.

Natalie shrinks and guilt washes over me that we're upsetting her, or worse, scaring her, as is reflected in her voice. "I should go. Your contract is on the table." She motions to the envelope and looks past me at the door.

With the skill I've practiced too many times with my brother, I bury my anger. "I overreacted. You deserve an explanation, but I need to clean up first. And you can't go..." I look uselessly out the window. "A mudslide took out the road just before Eggplant Canyon. I got caught in the edge of it. My car's a loss. I had to walk home."

"What?" they say in unison.

"There's no way out. You can stay here until they get the road cleared. We'll figure it out, I just need to get cleaned up first. Just don't touch her again, Jefferson." I take a step then decide against slogging mud through my immaculate house.

"Gotcha, I won't even stay in the same room as her unless you're here to chaperone," Jefferson says, presumably hearing the threat of castration in my voice.

I motion to my pants. "I'm going to have to strip down right here."

The number of times I've dreamed of stripping down with Natalie is so high I sometimes think she's really mine. And every damn time, I chastise myself for the naughty things I do to her. She's far too young and innocent.

Presuming they'll turn away if they want to, I slide my belt through the buckle and yank it from around my waist.

The weight of her gaze calls to me. I lift my eyes. She's staring. The softness of her features is highlighted by her hair falling in waves around her face. In the office, her bun keeps a professional, no-nonsense edge to her look.

My heart beats faster. My cock thickens. The financial institution we work for has stringent rules about fraternizing. Not a single one of those rules matters to me right now.

My brother disappears while Natalie remains in place, the only part of her that's moved is her jaw, which has fallen open ever so slightly.

I imagine that if I was close enough, her breaths could warm my neck while I hold her body against mine. My fingers would drag through her hair, down her back, and curve around her luscious ass. A not-so-gentle squeeze would make her breath hitch.

The ache in my balls anchors me to the actual moment that's playing out, which is even better than my fantasy. Wrapping my belt around my hand, another flicker of imagination has me wanting to bind her hands. Her breath hitches when she looks at the leather strap, but that's for another day. Maneuvering the button of my slacks, I loosen my pants and accept that I've become a show.

I click my zipper down a few notches, and I can't decide if I'm humored by Natalie staring, or if I'm going to try to make something of it.

A few more notches and I'm losing the ability to keep my cock from responding. Natalie's always had the hot secretary vibe, and I've never wanted to be the clichéd boss abusing his power, which is why I barely allow myself to look at her, handling as much business as possible electronically or over the phone.

Admittedly, I'm selfish. She's an incredible admin, one I'll never be able to replace. But the other factor is that I'd lose my shit if she worked for anyone but me. I'm protecting her.

I've long since wondered if her innocence was for show, but as she eats up every click of my zipper, and the increasing angle my cock is tenting my slacks, her innocence becomes less of a question, which only makes me harder.

I'm normally the untie-your-shoes-and-slide-them-off kind of guy, but with all of this mud, and my raging erection, I kick them off, shuck my pants carefully over my hardened cock, and watch Natalie's eyes go wide.

My underwear is stretched to its limit. I rub a hand over my cock to take the edge off, but it's not my hand I long for. Her delicate fingers, with those pretty manicured nails would look divine wrapped around my shaft.

If I don't get out of this room, I'm going to get us fired...but only if one of us tells. Fuck. That's a dangerous game to play, more so for her than me. I've been with the company for fifteen years. She's only been there a few months. I've seen how this plays out, and it's never fair.

How am I supposed to deal with her being trapped in my house? I could send her to her brothers' house, which is next door. They're the reason I hired her, but they'd failed to tell me she would steal my fucking heart. If either of them had shown me a picture, I would have asked her for a date instead of a resumé.

There's no fucking way I'm sending her next door. Now the question is to figure out how to keep her here and not regret it. Some guys might not want to piss off their neighbors by fucking their sister, but we're all adults.

With any luck, the shower won't just clean my body, but will also take care of my dirty thoughts. I ignore the fact that my dream girl is staring at my cock. "I better hit the shower."

Stripping my socks off, gathering my mess of clothes, and hoping there's enough cold water to talk the big guy down, I do the right thing and leave the room.

Four

Natalie

When I finally pull out of the erection enchantment, I retrieve my purse from my car and dial my brother, Nathan. No, our parents weren't very creative when it came to names. My half-brother, Carson, who also lives next door, got lucky that our mom hadn't thought of the matching name thing when he was born.

How long had I stared at my boss's erection? And why did he have one? I have so many questions about sex, and there's no one I'd rather have help me answer them than Mister Adams.

Other than *the other* Mister Adams.

How are there two of these perfect men walking the earth? I hang up the call before Nathan answers.

Was it totally cringy that I ogled my boss in his moment of despair? I hadn't even asked about his car or the mudslide...I'm not normally so insensitive.

Mindlessly staring out the window, I'm alone, a huge emotional letdown from the moments I had with each of the

Adams men moments before. But as I grasp for sanity, the ache between my legs and in my chest cloud my judgment.

Lincoln is as organized and tidy at home as he is in the office, which allows me to easily find his cleaning products. Cloud cover builds again, so I flip on the light, kick my shoes off by the front door, and busy myself with cleaning the mud he tracked in.

My phone rings. It's my reprieve, Nathan returning my call, but after an awkward conversation, I surmise that he doesn't want me at his house. Something's definitely up. If I wasn't trapped on the opposite side of the mudslide from my best friend, I'd go to her place. Rather than question my lack of options, I accept it as another nudge from the universe.

I make a risqué decision. Risqué coming from someone who recently turned old enough to order alcohol in a bar but has never done anything more than kissing and clothed contact.

It's as if an act of god trapped me in a situation that has an element of safety while offering an opportunity to explore a side of me I've never been comfortable with. I'm going to pursue whatever this is with my boss's twin.

Still on my knees, I stuff the last dirty paper towel into the plastic bag I'm using for trash when footfalls stop behind me.

The vulnerability of being on my hands and knees with my ass pointed at my boss takes a backseat to the heat pooling between my legs. I wish I was one of those sexy-minded women who would add a little wiggle to her hips. I'm not.

Instead, I sit on my heels and look over my shoulder.

The smolder in his eyes incinerates every last word I planned on saying about cleaning up. I'm not sure how a look, no matter how smoldering, can make me sweat, but I'm at least glistening.

He's even taller and more commanding from this angle. My face is way too close to his hip height. But it's the sweat pants, fitted t-shirt, and wet tousled hair that leave me so weak I'm not sure I can stand.

He's a man of impeccable tailoring and grooming, never a hair or stitch out of place.

"Thank you for cleaning that up, Miss Moore."

The most breathless ever "you're welcome" whisps from my lips. There's no air left in my lungs to tell him to call me Natalie.

Jefferson comes out of wherever he'd been hiding but doesn't leave as much distance as Lincoln kept. My head, while angled at my boss, rolls to the other side as I drift into a fantasy of these carbon copy gods teaching me all the things I've missed.

The awkward motion, and possible lightheadedness, cause me to tip. I slap a hand to the ground, highlighting my bobble, but as embarrassment tries to creep through me, Jefferson's hand is on my shoulder, his strong fingers working their way under my arm, his other hand reaching around to help me stand.

The contact, the security of it, the lingering moment, and the sense that his efforts were much more than simple assistance, fortify my decision to accept this opportunity for the gift that it is.

Does he understand what he's doing to me? Do guys like him have a sixth sense for fresh meat? Is that a horrible way to think about myself, or him?

I can't be anything but doe-eyed as I stare up at him.

"Are you okay, Miss Moore?" The seduction in the way he draws out my name makes me question if I'm already in over my head.

Hands grip my waist, even more firm and secure than Jefferson's, which are still on my upper arms.

Lincoln. The dampness in my panties is joined by an ache in my core. The heat from their bodies consumes me from both sides, but I want more than heat, I want pressure. I want words whispered in my ear, hands caressing my body, and lips stealing kisses from everywhere I've never been kissed.

The ache in my core twists into a knot that's being pulled at both ends, tighter and tighter. Sanity and lines drawn by my workplace no longer matter.

"Are you okay?" Lincoln whispers, his mouth so close to my ear. Can he read my thoughts?

"You looked dizzy." Jefferson steps closer.

Passing out won't further this fantasy. Breathe.

It helps. I lift my hands to Jefferson's waist, trailing them upward, stopping on his chest. My words are cut off by the contours my fingers memorize. Another breath.

"I'm fine now, thank you."

"You better sit down." Lincoln's hands around my waist pull me backward, guiding me away from his brother.

He leads me to the sofa, holds my hand as I sit, and just when I think he's taking the seat next to me, he clears his throat and moves to the nearby chair.

What should I make of that? I don't know. But when Jefferson sits next to me, a mere inch between us, and slings his arm behind me, it no longer matters. While I can't cross a line with my boss, his brother is a line I can definitely straddle.

A boom rattles the windows a split second before the lights go out. Reflexively, I lean into Jefferson. His arm tightens around my back, gripping my arm, and in the shuffle, his finger grazes the side of my breast.

Does he understand why I shudder? He slips his finger back a half inch but gives me no reason to move away. He's protecting me, and I *more than* like it.

Five

Lincoln

A flashlight and a long-burn-time emergency candle are all I have to ward off the darkness. The power rarely goes out and normally, I'm the only one here so that's enough. What irony that on the night I have two guests, I also have no electricity.

Finishing up the call to the power company, I return to the living room. The flame from the candle isn't a lot, but it is enough to see how close my twin and my admin are sitting. Touching. Taking advantage of the darkness? Seriously? My guests are going to fuck under my roof?

The odd lighting could be an excuse for the irritation that surely shows in my expression. I've clenched my jaw so tightly it hurts.

I set the candle down so I don't crush the container and send burning fuel all over my living room. I've held myself back from Natalie, respected corporate policy, respected her autonomy in the workplace...for what?

So she can shack up with my identical twin while we're trapped under my roof?

Anger seethes through me.

His thumb brushes over her cheek. She's giggling about something. Do they even notice I came into the room?

"I talked to a rep at the power company. They're not sure how soon they can fix the power. A transformer blew, but it's in Eggplant Canyon and with the mudslide the repair crews can't get to it."

"Everything will be fine." Jefferson's fucking laid-back attitude has grated on my nerves ever since he lost custody of his kid and practically checked out of having responsibility.

The flickering flame turns Natalie and Jefferson into an old movie, offering a stuttered vision of him touching her while she looks up at him adoringly. Does she see me when she looks at him? Is the thing between them physical? Or does she prefer his casual attitude over my control?

"Yeah, everything will be fine because I have plenty of food in the pantry, and I'll take the couch so Natalie has a bed to sleep in." It's my surefire way to separate them and make sure she's cared for.

"It's okay, Mister Adams, Jefferson offered to do that already." She giggles.

First names and giggles. She's already closer to him than I've been with her in the months she's worked right outside of my office. The notion gets under my skin, but the mission of separating them is accomplished. I can live with that.

"I'll get sheets and a blanket for you."

"You don't have to. Your sweet little admin is making your life easier long after the workday is over. She wants to share my bed."

My chest tightens, constricting my ability to talk, which is good since I'd tell him to keep his hands off my girl. What grown-up reason can I think of that they can't share a bed?

His hand slides onto her thigh. I'm about to blow. How do I get him to stop touching her? If I want to respect her autonomy, don't I have to respect a choice that I have no say in?

Fuck.

"That's not a good idea."

"What?" My brother asks as if he can't remember that he just said he was going to sleep with my admin.

"I'll take the couch. Natalie takes my bed. You stay in the guest room."

"I...well, we were..." Natalie can't quite bring herself to say something, and if she can't say it, she shouldn't be doing it in my extremely biased, possessive, pissed-off opinion.

"Natalie and I are going to work on a little project. Sharing a room will be perfect." Jefferson's vague statement insults me. Like I don't understand what sharing a bed with a gorgeous, giggling woman or working on a project means.

Give me a fucking break. The jealousy that's been threaded through our lives tightens itself around my chest. I've worked on a ton of projects with Natalie, and never did a single one make her giggle, require me to put my hands on her, or cause her to look up at me with her big doe-eyes.

But I will be the bigger man. I will hold a place of respect in her world. I won't ever let her down.

"Natalie, my offer stands, my bed is yours, just say the word." That came out closer to the truth than I'd intended. I try to cover. "Whatever happens between you and my brother won't have any bearing on our working relationship, is that clear?"

"Yes, Mister Adams." The way she lowers her voice haunts me.

There are so many other statements I long to hear that response to. The weight of the situation is nearly unbearable. I consider declaring that there will be no fucking or anything akin to that under my roof, but the last thing I want to do is treat her like a child.

I don't want to be the stick-in-the-mud. Work requires me to make harsh decisions. That's not what I want in my house. But *fuck*, I want her.

Watching her snuggle up to my brother, my cock is thickening. It could be me. It should be me. If only she hadn't been given a choice. I've never hated Jefferson more than at this moment.

"I'm going to bed." I storm out of the room, angling my body in the dim light to keep them from seeing my erection.

Six

Natalie

I worry my lower lip as my boss strides out of the room. Despite his declaration, it seems that whatever's happening between Jefferson and me is already affecting my work relationship with Lincoln.

It all just feels so right. I've been wanting to meet a guy I felt comfortable learning about sex with, and possibly getting the whole virginity thing knocked out. Jefferson's perfect. I've been physically attracted to his twin, my boss, since my first day of employment, and the more I got to know Lincoln, the more I understood how reputable he is, which makes his brother all the more appealing.

Basically, I get to explore my fantasy about my boss with a carbon copy of him, thus I'm not breaking the rules.

When my boss is out of sight, I watch the candle flame for a minute and wonder if I'm playing with fire. "Maybe we shouldn't do this."

Jefferson's gentle caress of my jaw guides my face up to his. "Why?"

I wait for him to say more but the sound of rain pelting the windows is all I get.

"My boss seems upset that we're sharing a bed...I mean, we can still do that, but the project I mentioned is a no-go."

His hand rests patiently against my cheek. "Your boss doesn't get to dictate your personal life. But I'll do anything for you...even call this off."

His words are what I tell myself I need to hear.

"That's what I want."

"Okay, then I won't misinterpret the way you look up at me with a faraway look in your eyes as attraction."

I force my traitorous eyes closed.

His hand lowers from my face and I should be able to think better when he's not touching me. His contact continues over the contour of my jaw and painstakingly slowly down my neck.

"And I won't teach you what it feels like to be kissed here."

Did my head just tip to the side? I should stop this.

His finger strokes inward and trails down the center of my chest, slowly again as his words seduce me.

"And there's no need for me to show you how kisses down your chest can make your breasts heave, you have that mastered with just the touch of my finger. Hmm...such a loss for me. I was looking forward to teasing my tongue between your beautiful breasts, then across the top of them."

35

His finger, his tongue...how far will he go with this non-lesson. My body is marked by the trail he takes, the first man to touch me in such a way. Even if this can never be, I'll never forget it.

"The luscious swell of your breasts must torture Lincoln every time he looks at you. I bet he can't stop himself from imagining how they would be more than he could fit in his large hand."

Is it normal to have electricity zing from my breast to my sex? Is there a nerve connecting them or something? Jefferson's hand, presumably the same size as Lincoln's, cradles my breast while his thumb passes back and forth over my nipple that's beading harder and harder with each stroke.

I hear my own breaths. I feel my chest rise and fall. I have no doubt he's the right guy to learn about sex with, except that pissing off my boss could cost me my job. My brother would be livid that I threw away the golden opportunity he finagled for me.

"There are so many more lessons I could teach you." He removes his hand from my body.

This is my chance to do the right thing. I'm sure I can find a sheet and blanket to use on the couch.

His fingers brush over my bare knee. My skirt rides up to just above my knees when I sit, and he's already exploring under the hem of my skirt.

"One of the most important lessons *someone* should teach you..."

When did he lean in? His breath warms my ear. That's a lesson in itself. My heart's cranking overtime. I have an uncanny desire to rip off his clothes. And I'm still trying to convince myself this is wrong.

"is that your lover should always make sure you're taken care of first."

A strange whimpering sound from me elicits a huff of a laugh from him. Then he continues.

"It's true. Guys can be ready in a heartbeat, even beats as fast as yours, and when a guy has a woman as incredible as you, there's no question he can be ready. But women need to be shown that they're treasured first, and when they're truly ready, everything will be more enjoyable."

I might break the mold then because this isn't taking me any time at all.

"You do know what I'm talking about, don't you?" His fingers tease up my thigh.

"Yes," I may or may not squeak out.

"Since you called off our sex lessons, I'm not your teacher, but my conscience would be put at ease if you explained—just so I don't have to worry that you would let a man treat you wrong."

"I won't let anyone treat me wrong."

His hand covers the top of my thigh. Dang it, another traitorous body part reveals itself to me as my other thigh shifts outward.

"You see, I'm worried. You let your boss into your personal life. I want to be sure you're aware of what your body can do. If you don't know, there's no shame in asking for one small lesson."

Oh. My. God. I'm going for it. "One lesson."

I duck my head and curl my lips in.

I hope I'm right, that it's a good thing that I'm wet. I think he'll like that. The slow slide of his hand between my thighs is followed by the backs of his fingers pushing against my opposite thigh, requesting more space.

My skirt will allow it. Will my conscience? Is it possible that my boss will walk back into the room at the exact same second the lights come on? Will he see me spread for his brother, not in the privacy of a bedroom, but brazenly on the sofa?

Will I regret this? Time will tell because I shift to open my legs.

A strained sound comes from Jefferson's chest. My legs may be open, but my eyes are not, allowing me the fantasy, the denial, and the crazy, unbelievable moment.

He barely slides his hand forward but extends a fingertip to brush over my panties. My wetness is more than I thought. My panties seem soaked. That's never happened.

"Oh, Baby Doll, this is how you can tell." I catch my use of the nickname, pause for a split second, and when she doesn't object, I continue. "When you're ready for sex, these sweet juices will help you take your lover's cock." He takes a deliberate inhale. "He'll be addicted to your scent from the first breath."

He withdraws his hand and leans his face back from my ear.

No. My body slumps. My eyes flutter open. I need him.

Inches from my disbelieving eyes, his finger is on his lips. The tip of his tongue drags over the pad. Breaths become huge, punctuated efforts. Then he presses his finger to my parted lips.

My scent is more intriguing than ever. A reaction to him? I want more. Leaning ever so slightly, I take his fingertip in my lips and suck.

Seven

Jefferson

I flop my arm over my head, blocking the flashes of lightning coming into the living room where I'm dutifully sleeping on the couch.

Faster than a Bugatti can do zero to sixty, Natalie went from sucking on my finger to standing at the far end of the couch with her hands clasped over her mouth.

She did tell me that she didn't want lessons and I'd pushed it, but damn, I thought I hooked her.

The secondary problem to the lightning is my erection. Aside from the reality that I would have prodded her all night if we were in the same bed, she had true concern for not upsetting Lincoln.

But even in the dim light, I'd seen in her eyes how much she wanted the lessons. It's not completely incredulous to me that a twenty-one-year-old hasn't had sex, it's the rest of her innocence that gets me. She hasn't done anything aside from lip kissing and over-the-clothes petting.

Telling myself that our fourteen-year age gap is too much hasn't helped my erection any. Telling myself not to let the lure of being her first, at so many things, cloud my judgment doesn't help either. And telling myself that my erection is somehow going to magically go away on its own is flat-out ridiculous.

Waiting a while to make sure everyone is down for the night, I head to the kitchen, grab a paper towel, and shuck my boxer brief to the tops of my thighs. I lean back against the granite countertop, rub the plentiful pre-cum over my cock, and stroke.

I try squeezing a little more than normal, but it's no substitute for her pussy. My mind runs wild with the lessons I almost got to give her. Who knows if they would have ended in actual sex, she wasn't sure about that, but she was sure about everything up to it.

The thing I'm having a harder time reconciling is why I felt so attracted to her, like we're meant to be together. When people say that they knew at their first meeting they were going to get married, I didn't believe it was possible. Now I can say, it's one of those things you don't understand until you experience it.

My balls tighten at the thought of marrying her. They're even tighter at the vision of her belly swollen with our baby.

Is fate cruel? Will I get hit with karmic interference for not being there for my son? Does it help that I have a plan to win back a place in his life?

Anger fuels my urgency. I stroke faster.

"Oh my!" a feminine voice cries out from the end of the hallway at the end of the kitchen. It's Natalie's. It's too much.

Even as her voice pushes me dangerously close to climax, I dare to look her direction. My intent is to let go of my shaft and apologize, but when I see her big eyes glued to my efforts, wicked desire consumes me.

I take in the swell of her tits and her beaded nipples perking through the oversized t-shirt that only has panties under it at most. Her bright peach painted toenails stand out against her pale skin in the dim lighting, and bare legs...damn they'd look good spread. Her hands brace in the doorway, her mouth agape, ready to take cock—or perhaps just out of surprise—the whole package of her makes me desperate to be the one to teach her.

I blow my load. Stream after stream that I wish were filling her womb splat on the tile floor while she watches. She steps forward but catches herself before making it more than one step.

Natalie's seen my erection. She's seen me stroke myself. She's seen me come. I've secured her as my student and secured multiple firsts for her. I want to beat my chest and roar to express the primal victories I'm celebrating, but my sweet doll isn't ready for that.

"Come here, Baby Doll." I drag my hand over my cock one last time.

Glancing over her shoulder, she says, "I should go to my room."

"You ready for another lesson? Want me to go with you?

Her head whips back to me. Her gaze shifts from my eyes to my cock that's still semi-hard to the mess on the floor to my hand. If she wanted to go to her room she would have. I'd never force myself on a woman, but with Natalie, I'm more than willing to force the issue that she's having a hard time admitting what she truly wants.

Hell, I already forced the issue by ejaculating for her.

"I won't ask why you want lessons, or why you're nervous about sex..." I shove my cock back in my underwear. "but the more you tell me, the better I can understand the best way to guide you."

"There's no big fancy reason. I was just too shy."

"You're not shy now, Baby Doll. You took a big long look at my cock. Let's do another lesson right here." I motion for her to come over.

She lowers her head, worries her lower lip, and looks at me from under her lashes. "My boss—"

"He won't fire you." I grab spray cleaner from under the sink and wipe up the floor while I try to put her worries at ease.

"How can you be sure?"

"Because he told me you're the best admin he's ever had."

"But you're his brother, will that make him mad?"

"Can you keep what we do separate from what you do with him?"

There's a pause. "Yes."

43

"Are you sure? You hesitated."

"It's just that you look the same. What if I…"

I nod, "You're attracted to him."

"Please don't tell him."

That stirs up unwelcome competition in me. "I'm happy to leave him completely out of this. And since we're being open and honest… We can be a thing. I'm not your boss, I'm just a guy who thinks you're the most amazing woman on the planet."

"You do? You barely know me."

"Call it a sixth sense, but I have every intention of pursuing you even if you don't want lessons." There are a couple of trickier things I don't explain. One is that in being an identical twin, there are things I sense about her through my brother. All good. The other is that he feels the same way about her as I do. Not so good, but he's strict about business relationships, which means he'll never go after her.

"Pursuing…as in dating?"

"I want to do a lot more than date you, but that's a good starting point. Will you give me a chance?"

Her smile lights up my world as she steps closer. "Will you give me a lesson?"

Eight

Natalie

The past couple of minutes are almost too much to process. The past couple of hours are just as surreal.

With each footstep, I'm closer to living out another of my fantasies I have of my boss. There's a mental row of file cabinets worth of fantasies, but making out with him...which is all I'm committing to right now, is a great start. Or should I say, a great continuation since a few others got moved to the completed drawer already?

Stopping beside him, I look up. They're staggeringly identical, but I've never been this close to Lincoln, and the closeness makes Jefferson seem taller, broader, hotter.

He pushes off the counter, faces me, and cups my head in his hands. Is it possible to feel like I belong to him? Maybe that's what he meant by his sixth sense comment.

"Baby Doll, let me be everything for you, not just while we're trapped here, but when the road is clear and we can go back into the world, into our regular lives. Tell me that you'll still be mine."

Swoon, bone liquefication complete. I'm not sure how I'm still standing. But he can't possibly mean what he said.

"That's a big promise. What if things don't work out? I might only be good at office work and not bedroom stuff."

A humored huff rumbles through him. "I don't have any doubts, Baby Doll, but if you're worried, no promises are necessary."

"Thanks." Is he perfect, or is it just my naïveté falling prey to a playboy? Either way, I've protected myself by not promising anything. I won't fall apart and cryo-preserve myself with Haagen Dazs if he moves on.

"Mind if I offered some of those lessons I mentioned earlier?" He trails the back of his fingers down my neck.

"That's a good place to start."

His eyes flit to my lips, and he catches my tongue wetting them. It makes him smile. He looks so handsome when he smiles, something Lincoln rarely does.

He leans slowly and his lips part. Mine follow suit until he's too close and I can't focus. It's too intense to look into his eyes, so I close mine and accept the first few pecks he puts on my lips.

I want more. I want him inside of me. He's driving me crazy with the slowness, and yet, I've given him every indication that I want to go slowly. Sliding my tongue between his lips, I give him permission to proceed to the next lesson.

Having his tongue inside of me changes me. We become one with each other at this superficial but important level. He lets me lead for a second then takes over, guiding me on our dance. Dipping me deeper and deeper into what we can be.

I don't need breath. I only need Jefferson. But when his kisses trail over my cheek and down my neck, new shivers race through me. A nip at my earlobe gives me a shudder, and the knot in my core tightens.

"Do you ever touch yourself?" he asks between kisses.

I shake my head no even though I have. How can he be so bold? Or am I even more naïve than I thought?

"Are you lying to me?" He takes my hand and cups it between my legs. "You've never put your hand here?"

I nod and pinch my eyes shut, shamed at being caught in a lie, and afraid that if I open them, I'll somehow break the spell.

The pressure of his hand on mine relents and he lifts his hand to stroke my hair. I let my hand linger a second.

"It's nothing to be ashamed of. It's healthy. Now open your eyes and tell me.

Is this part of the lesson? I flutter my eyes open and the darkness helps me not feel so vulnerable. "I've touched myself."

His eyes are tender as they own me. "Fuck yeah, Baby Doll, that's hot."

Surprise causes me to suck in a large awkward inhale. His statement is one I never imagined anyone telling me.

He tries to lace his fingers in mine, but I'm so overflowing with sexual tension, I can't navigate the finger separation required.

"Are you nervous?"

"Yes."

"Do you trust me?"

The level of trust I have with him is weird. It's like I know him, but I don't really. "I do. I'm just all wound up with everything..."

"I can help you unwind."

His stare holds so much more than his simple statement.

"How?" Did I really ask that? I feel like such a dork, even though it's a fair question.

He leans into my ear like he did earlier. "Let me make you come."

My head drops against his and we both turn, morphing into a kiss, a hunger, a promise of how he'll take care of me. I'm a goner.

Jefferson is my future, no matter how complicated that might be. His hand slides between my legs, lifting the t-shirt. This is the first time I've been without panties when I'm in the presence of a man.

His fingers slide over my sex, coating themselves in my juices.

"Baby Doll, where are your panties?"

"I didn't expect to stay here, so I don't have extras. I washed them in the sink and have them hanging to dry."

"You're going to make such a good…"

What was he going to say? Never mind. His fingers press the devil's doorbell and I answer with moans. It feels so good, but we're so close. Where do I look? His chest, the floor, his face, out the window? I close my eyes.

My pleasure is interrupted when he lets his fingers rest. He explains, "Why don't you turn around, lean against me, then you don't have to worry about where to look."

Was my awkwardness that noticeable? Kudos to him for the great idea. He spreads his legs, positions me between them, then leans me against his solid body. One of his hands returns to my sex while the other massages my breast.

The combination is insanely stimulating.

"That's right, Baby Doll, surrender to me. You're so fucking beautiful."

I'm struggling to keep my moans quiet so I don't wake up my boss, but also because of the sweet things Jefferson is whispering in my ear.

"Let go, I've got you."

Everything my parents taught me about sex being a tool for reproduction is washing away with the storm. There's too much pleasure to restrict this to baby making.

"You feel what you do to me." He shifts his hips to press his erection into my backside.

"What the fuck?" It's Jefferson's voice but not the sweet whispers, it's full of shock, and it's from too far away.

Oh no! Jefferson must figure it out about the same time I do. He wraps his arms around me, preventing me from running away, but also smooths a hand down, making sure I'm covered.

I stare at the ground. Humiliation is the new emotion. Isn't that the one right before you get fired for lewd acts? I try to wiggle free, but Jefferson won't let go. Is he using me to hide his erection, which hasn't gone down with the intrusion?

"I'm sorry, Mister Adams."

"I can't believe..." My boss doesn't finish his statement.

"Don't be mad at her. I assured Natalie you understand the limits of your control over her."

My boss strides closer, sending my heart rate skyrocketing.

Jefferson tightens his grip.

Mister Adams is too close, and I like it too much. I gasp at my thought. My fantasies, which had only contained one of him, suddenly invite themselves to pretend I could have two of him. Is the ache for an orgasm causing me to lose all decorum?

He hooks a finger under my chin, the same as his brother had done. Electricity zips through my body. Too many hands, too much contact...we've always maintained our professional space.

"Natalie, be honest with me." My boss, using a lower tone than normal, telling me to be honest is seductive enough. The compromising position of his brother's erection pressed into my backside sends my imagination into a frenzy. Is there a good possible outcome? I have a feeling I'm going to want to lie.

"Okay."

"You barely know him. Are you pretending you're with me?"

Oh fuck. Am I in trouble? It sure doesn't sound like it.

"You look a lot alike."

Jefferson's fingers dig into my sides. What does that mean? Lincoln's expression darkens. What does anything mean?

I try to explain. "You're my boss. He's not."

Lincoln drags his thumb over my lips. "Are you saying you'd let me do what I caught him doing to you?"

This is a dangerous question. My pulse is pounding in my ears. If I make either one of them mad will this all be over?

He lowers his hand, taking mine, holding it preciously.

"If you weren't my boss...I would." Will I regret that?

Lightning strikes and thunder rattles the windows instantly. I'd swear I could feel the electrical charge in the air, but we had it the second my boss sandwiched me against his brother.

I brace myself for whatever he's about to say.

Nine

Lincoln

My world was shaken today, literally when the mudslide crashed down the side of the mountain, the fringes of it encircling my car, and figuratively when I got an erection in front of my admin who'd been bent over cleaning my floor.

I tried to maintain control. I followed the rules and denied the attraction, the pull between us, and even left the room when I saw Natalie snuggled up to my brother.

But walking into the kitchen, seeing his hand between her legs, eliciting muffled cries of pleasure, I broke.

"I won't ask you to do anything, or break any rules you want to leave in place, but Natalie, I want you."

"A little late, bro." The irritation in Jefferson's voice tells me he's ready for a fight. Will I win because Natalie knows and trusts me, or will Jefferson win because there are no rules around him?

Or can we let Natalie win...and find a way to let her have both of us? Am I kidding myself that this is possible? What will happen when we go back to work?

"I have a proposition. No one has to know what happens here, and no one should have to make a choice. Do you think you can handle both of us, Natalie?"

"I have no idea." She sounds truly baffled.

I lift my eyes to Jefferson's. "Want to help her find out?"

His answer is clear to me before he says anything. He wants her for himself, but he ultimately wants to make her happy. She sees me when she looks at him.

"My Baby Doll wanted me to teach her the basics of sex, but I'm game for higher education." He kisses the top of her head. "We'll treat you right."

"Okay."

"You were learning about sex? Which lesson were you on?" I stroke a finger over the shirt I let her borrow.

"She's never had an orgasm with a man."

Is that true? I search her eyes and suspect it is. Being the first man to please her swells my chest. It has to be me. It's like fate helped me interrupt just in time because by the sounds of it, she'd been about to come when I walked in.

"I really need one." Her tone is so wanton, a far cry from the soft yet formal version of her in the office.

"I can handle it." Jefferson tries to lay claim but I can't let him.

"I'm sure you can, but you could also strip her shirt off, and get those pretty titties I've dreamed of on full display so I can watch you play with them while I eat her out."

In a flurry, the shirt is gone and her beautiful, creamy white breasts and rosy beaded nipples are beacons in the moonlight. The curves of her naked body give me pause at how well I can see her. The storm subsided and moonlight streams in.

Resting my hands on her hips, I have to catch my breath. She's everything I dreamed of. Everything I've jacked off to. Everything I want except for a belly swollen with my child. Yeah, my imagination ran a little wild. Yet here she is, and there's not a single condom in my house.

My brother's hands snake around her body working her breasts, pressing them upward creating even more fullness. Damn. I hope he didn't bring any condoms. I *need* to ride her bare.

Closing the small space between us, my erection tips out against my pajama pants enough that it touches her. A surge of pre-cum gives me a tiny bit of relief. Wishing I could bury myself balls deep in her, I kiss the angel who's been hiding out as my admin. She's softer and more ready than I expected.

My brother nudges the backs of his hands against my chest, and I take the cue. Lowering myself to my knees, I trail my hands down her legs. I've merely moved from kissing one piece of heaven to another.

Her scent is divine. When it lingers on my lips, it will breathe life into me with every inhale. I don't have to rely on that while my tongue slides between her lips. Her sweet juices coat me. Her moans are angelic, and for all that I want to drag this out and give her endless pleasure, I'm dying to make her come.

Sucking and lapping at her clit, I savor the contrast of her soft, luscious mounds with Jefferson's large, tanned hands. It's erotic, and I'm about to come from watching, and of course, having my mouth on her pussy.

I let up just enough to lift one of her legs over my shoulder and let her get used to the new position. When her moans deepen, I go full force again, picking up the rhythm and tongue flicks she liked best.

How can I want to be everything for her and be willing to share her at the same time? My brother and I have never done anything like this. My cock is rock hard.

My angel is most definitely a centerfold, in my mind. Forever. I shake off the technical difficulties the real world will offer. The small pumps of her hips against my face ruin me.

Then she comes undone and bathes my mouth in her release. She is an angel. My angel. Our angel. I lick and lick, taking her through wave after wave of pleasure.

We're made for each other. Our work relationship was a stepping stone to bring her into my life. The mudslide was another stone to force us together. Jefferson is simply a final step to bring her to me.

If anything was ever meant to be...it's us.

Ten

Natalie

My eyes flutter open, my body slowly gaining consciousness as the events of the previous evening re-populate my brain. I'm sprawled across my boss's bed after one of the best night's sleep I've ever had.

But I'm alone.

Does that mean something? Hopefully, the only message is that I slept so hard I didn't notice Lincoln and Jefferson get up. I roll onto my side, squeezing my exhausted thighs together. The guys satisfied me over and over again, between snuggles and conversations, but they said we shouldn't have sex right away.

Not that they didn't want to...they'd been quick to point out. They just didn't want to rush things more than we already had. All three of us felt a bit of disbelief at our attraction and comfort with each other.

The floor-to-ceiling window gives ample view of the pillowy, dark clouds looming across the top of the mountain. They appear ready to unleash another downpour. I groan as my thoughts segue into the numerous times the twins made me come, and the fact that I drenched their faces, fingers, and shafts, although only as I rocked myself over their lengths.

It had been enough to make Lincoln come. As much as I wanted him inside of me, I'd popped my eyes open when his groans got really deep, and I got to see the white streams shoot onto his chest and belly.

It's hard to compare it to Jefferson masturbating in the kitchen, which had been totally hot, and totally new to me. The swell of Lincoln's cock under my sex, knowing I was the reason, had me addicted to watching them come.

It's no wonder sex, money, and power get intertwined. Money and power go hand in hand so obviously. It was the sex thing I didn't understand, but I feel powerful with the small assortment of things we've done.

The desire to be filled lingers even after all of the orgasms. If penetration is half as good as I expect it will be, I'll have these guys at my mercy...and I'll willingly be at theirs.

Now that we've had a chance to sleep on our wild night, I pray they haven't changed their minds, particularly my boss. It wouldn't be the same without him. My moment alone with Jefferson was brief but good. When Lincoln joined in, I was on instant overload in the best way possible.

What a grand first adventure.

I think I did fine other than closing my eyes. It's not that I want to shut them out, there's just so much emotion and sensation that the visual is distracting to me, which might be the stupidest thing a woman could ever say when getting claimed by identical gods.

I need to go find them and see where we stand. I roll away from the window and study Lincoln's bedroom. Good thing he has a king-size bed so we all fit. His decorations are sparse and elegant, grays and black, contrasted by splashes of dark blue in a throw blanket, lamp, and massive geode painted on the wall. The lines in it are so crisp and the shine off the different angles so bright and realistic, I thought it was wallpaper.

But I'm stalling. The chance of getting to wake up to this more than another morning or two remains to be determined. I head to the en suite bathroom that's bigger than the living room of my apartment and decide that any time I spend trapped in Eggplant Canyon is a gift, and I'll gladly enjoy every second of it.

The real world with its real jobs with real rules awaits.

Giddiness invigorates me when I spy my bobby pins on the bathroom counter. They're no longer useful, but they're also no longer the mangled mess I'd created of them. Jefferson shaped them into two intertwined hearts. I tap them to my lips for a kiss then return them while I get ready.

I consider how much I'll be able to fix myself up with the limited makeup I have in my purse, and laugh at myself for thinking my mother would be horrified that I wasn't better prepared for an emergency. My makeup selection is far from the most horrific thing she would point to right now as I open my boss's drawer to find a new t-shirt to wear since the one last night must still be in the kitchen.

There's no question that a young administrative assistant who's been at the company a couple of months is less valuable than a financial guru who's been there for years. Not that either of us plans on saying anything.

But that was yesterday when Lincoln's nerves had been run ragged by narrowly escaping the mudslide, presuming his car was totaled, and catching his brother and admin in a compromising position.

I won't take it personally if he comes to his senses today.

They must hear me because they're looking when I round the corner to the kitchen. The smiles on their mouths, the hunger in their eyes, and the lack of shirts on their chests fill me with warmth and excitement. We exchange pleasantries but I opt to stay at the other end of the kitchen from them.

It might be easier to ask where we stand before I get too close.

"You were sleeping pretty hard. Do you feel okay?" Jefferson asks.

Lincoln holds up a bowl of yogurt and berries and nods at it. I shake my head.

"I'm not sure how to answer how I feel. Well-rested, yes. Mind-blown, yes." I hesitate when the bravado I thought I could work up to fails to manifest. Passing up this golden opportunity would be foolish.

"And..." Jefferson leads.

Lincoln's expression is tenser than Jefferson's, which is pretty much how he normally looks.

I lean against the doorway. "I'm just going to come out and ask...Can we have sex today?"

Lincoln's head whips toward me. Jefferson's spoon falls from his hands, clattering against the bowl.

"So I take it, the lessons were satisfactory?" Jefferson asks.

"They were enough to leave me wanting more. I have an IUD. I'm totally clean. And...I don't want to have a bad first time like I hear so many girls talk about. After yesterday, I don't see how it could possibly be bad with either of you. Please."

Lincoln studies me, his dark expression leaving me at a loss as to what's going on in his mind.

Jefferson groans. "Did you just ask us to please have sex with you?"

"Yes. If you're willing." I force a smile and realize that I'm toying with the hem of the shirt, which means it's pulled up my thigh, not quite enough to expose me and my pantie-less sex, but close.

"Baby Doll, when you first told me you were a virgin, I thought it might be a game, but getting to know you last night, I believed you, which is the only reason I can believe you don't understand how badly I want to fill you with my cock. Hell yeah, I'll make love to you."

Lincoln raises an eyebrow. Did he catch the "make love" comment too? I don't want to make too much of a turn-of-phrase but my heart is doing flip-flops.

Reggae music comes out of nowhere, drawing our attention to Jefferson as he reaches for his phone. "Fuck, I have to take this, but I'll take *you* as soon as I'm done."

He strides to the window as he answers. His back is to us, leaving my boss and me hanging on the comment.

"Come here," Lincoln says, reminiscent of when Jefferson said it to me last night.

I pad over to him, comforted by his outstretched hand. He threads our fingers together, bringing them up to his lips for a kiss.

"Breaking workplace rules isn't something I'm comfortable with, but I'm also a realist, and there's no way I can deny what's happening between us. If we move forward, we can't breathe a word of this to anyone."

"Okay." That doesn't work long term, but maybe we'll be like most couples and not last. That thought can be put in the utterly ridiculous file, but I suppose that's what most people think at first.

"Give me time to figure it out, and I promise I'll make this right."

"I'm not worried." Secretly, I can think of a million reasons to be worried, but what I feel for my boss and his twin washes it all away. And I suppose if someone were to put a picture of us in the online gossip group in town, we could claim I'm with Jefferson, as long as both guys aren't in the picture.

He shifts his hands to my butt, grabbing both cheeks, pulling me into his erection, hoisting me up, then sitting in a wooden chair in the breakfast nook with me on his lap.

I'm sure he's keenly aware that I'm splayed for him, that my wet lady bits are soaking his underwear. This position, except with him laying was how I'd watched him come. My nipples bead so hard they hurt.

"Have you thought about how you want to do it your first time?"

"Everything we did was amazing."

"Were there any positions that felt particularly right?"

I love how open they are with sex talk. It frees me to pretend that it's normal, as opposed to being brand new. They're teaching me in so many ways.

"I liked it when I was on you last night, when we both came at the same time. But now that I'm sitting in your lap, I like that because you're close to me. I can hold onto your shoulders."

"You want your first time right here?"

"Yeah." Why not? We have plenty of time to explore other positions.

"Hang on." He stands me up, strips his underwear, springs his rock-hard, bigger-than-I-remembered cock free, then pulls me onto his lap again.

He doesn't enter me yet, just pulls me against his erection. Pre-cum leaks from his tip and I'm already soaked, but I let him slow me down. Deep passionate kisses send me into the fantasy world where I'm all lust and feels.

He pumps his cock against me, stimulating my clit, knotting my first orgasm of the morning. I'm trying not to interrupt Jefferson's call, and let out a silent scream when my orgasm splinters me.

The drag of my shirt up my body helps me drift back to the breakfast nook. A cough from the window draws my attention. Jefferson's watching, and I can't tell if the strain in his expression is from the call, or from not being in the chair about to get laid.

He's being very careful with his wording but doesn't leave the room. Something has him worried.

Lincoln lifts me, positioning me over his tip. "Tell me if you're uncomfortable or need to stop for any reason."

"I will." I shift my attention to him but the intensity in his eyes unnerves me. He's watching for any sign I'm not into it. That's good, but I have to look away. I lock eyes with Jefferson. My body's on display. I'm about to lose my virginity to my boss. Hopefully, I won't lose my job too.

The push of his swollen cock head past my lips has me panting. The stretch as he enters me further is a melee of pain and pleasure.

"You okay, Angel?"

"Yes. I can do this."

He holds my body against his, rubs a finger over my clit, and thrusts.

My world spirals out of control. Being full of his cock is the most satisfying sensation ever. My arms are tight around his neck. My walls contract mercilessly on his shaft. I have to move.

Instinctively rocking my body on his shaft, my mind replays the beauty of his cock spraying ropes of cum. How will that feel inside of me?

What is Jefferson thinking? Sex is a drug. It's powerful. It's all-consuming. For a brief moment, before I totally lose myself to it, I open my eyes to make sure Jefferson's still watching.

Eleven

Jefferson

Fucking hell. My baby doll is riding my brother like a damn pro. I hate myself for barely focusing on what my lawyer's saying.

Getting custody of my son is the most important thing in my world, but Natalie enchants me. She would be the perfect mother, or stepmother, to my son and the rest of the babies I want to make with her. She's sweet and considerate and wants to have lots of kids according to our sleepy snuggle talk.

And if it wasn't for this call, I'd be the one putting a baby in her right now. Fuck her IUD. I'll pull it out myself.

The call. I try to focus. The fact that I haven't hung up is the fringe of sanity I use to remind myself that I have my priorities straight.

My cock hardens so fast, I lose my train of thought and have to ask the lawyer to repeat himself. So be it if he hears her come, I can't walk away from this. Can't miss my baby doll having sex for the first time. It should have been me.

Her closed eyes have my balls squeezing pre-cum out. She's so fucking pretty, innocent, and perfect. Then she opens her eyes and stares straight at me.

I drop my phone.

She smiles but it's quickly overtaken by the moans she's struggling to keep quiet. I shove my underwear down while retrieving my phone, apologize to my lawyer, and shamelessly stroke myself.

Baby Doll leans back, letting me see her big titties bounce while she rides Lincoln. My entire body is ready to blow.

"You're doing so fucking good, Angel. My cock's never been this hard." Are his hushed words rubbing it in? It makes her smile so I'll get over it.

"It feels so good."

"I'm ready to fill you up, Angel. Are you ready to come?"

"I'm...so...close." Her eyes alternate between falling shut and watching me.

Then she bites her lower lip and furrows her brow. I tell my lawyer I have to go, and hang up. Am I fit to be a parent?

"I'm off the phone, Baby Doll. Don't hold back. Let that orgasm wreck you."

Her fingers dig into Lincoln's shoulders, her head tips back, and she cries out with her release. Breaths sneak in between each moan. I'm barely hanging on. I can't fathom how he hasn't nutted. Then he does.

His growl rumbles like thunder through the room. His fingers dig into her hips and pump her up and down while her body's falling limp.

"Fuck." His single word sums up the intensity of what I'm watching. Do they have any idea how hot they are?

With half-lidded eyes focused on my hand stroking back and forth, she says, "Don't waste that."

Holy. Fucking. Hell. I rip my hand from my cock and deprive myself of stimulation because one more touch...breath...anything and I'll blow.

"I'm ready for my next lesson," she says breathlessly.

I fling a chair around, right next to theirs, drop myself onto it, and reach around her waist, working with the two of them to get her off of Lincoln's cock and hover her over mine while their joined release drips onto me.

"I love you, Baby Doll." Damn, that was supposed to be something clever about lessons.

Her smile is small but sincere as I plunge her onto my aching shaft and hold her still. I'm home. She's destined to be the mother of my kids. And I'm ready to fuck her so hard and fast my cum knocks her IUD loose.

"I need you, Baby. Is this okay?" I circle her clit with my thumb.

She whispers "yes" as I take her beaded nipple into my mouth. Her walls tighten around my shaft. I'm barely hanging on.

At the first sign of her body tensing, I bounce her on my shaft. Is there a lesson in this? For her? Probably. For me? I learn that there is such a thing as perfection, and that having my twin involved isn't a competition, he completes us.

Seconds later she milks me and I lose all sense of where she begins and I end. I coat her insides while our combined release drenches my lap.

Lincoln takes one of her hands, kisses it, and reaches over to rub her back.

Pumping my hips into her until my strength is spent, I hold her against my body, her head nestling on my shoulder.

"You're mine, Baby Doll. You're so fucking mine."

"You forgetting something?" My brother's voice is dangerously close to my ear. "She's ours. You're all ours, Angel."

The moment is too perfect to risk uttering another "I love you." Saying it again might pressure her if she's still blindsided by what we have. She might not understand how special this is, and I shut out the thought badgering the back of my mind that this might simply be lessons to her.

I can't risk custody of my kid over a woman who's using me for educational purposes. I have to keep my head straight, but right now the only thing clear is that I love her.

Twelve

Natalie

Our sexy bubble bursts when my phone rings. It's time that I would normally be showing up for work.

The main secretary is checking on me. "We expected Mister Adams to be gone. The Eggplant Canyon mudslide made big news in Peach Bottom Valley, but you're not here either. You're always prompt."

"I was dropping a contract off at his house. You know, he's my brothers' neighbor, so I was in the neighborhood when it happened."

Lincoln busies himself as I navigate the conversation away from exactly where I spent the night, to questions about what I had scheduled for the day and whether I'll be able to work remotely.

Apparently, Lincoln hadn't given me as much space as I thought, because he holds his laptop up and quietly says that I can use it for the day.

By the time I wrap up with her, Lincoln has taken a shower and fired up his desktop computer. Bummer since I'd hoped for a lesson on the infamous shower sex.

I walk up behind Jefferson, who's on the phone, I think with the same person as earlier, and wrap my arms around him.

He pats my hands and says to the other person. "Give me a few minutes, I'll be there."

Then just as quickly as he'd hung up earlier, he cuts the call off, spins around, hugs and kisses me, then peels my arms from his waist.

"Where are you going? Did they get the road open?"

"Not yet. I'm meeting a neighbor."

"Oh, you sounded so serious, and look so serious, I thought it was a business call."

"Sort of." He pushes me away and the distance feels like more of a chasm than an arm's length.

"Is your neighbor helping with your new security company?"

His jaw flexes and he inhales. "We'll talk later."

Such a tiny statement that emphasizes how huge the chasm is. I asked for lessons and I'm getting them. For example, people are prone to saying things in the heat of passion, that they might not say otherwise. I unwind his "I love you" from my heart. Lesson learned.

"I didn't mean to pry."

"I'll explain later when we have more time. I have to go." He pecks the top of my head then rushes out of the room so fast it's unlikely he hears my agreement.

What did I expect? Giving myself a mental shake, I head for the shower alone.

On my way, I veer toward Lincoln, who's on the phone. He waves me off and puts a finger to his lips. That's right, I'm a secret.

Yep, I've officially mastered the 'back to reality' lesson. I don't fault him for the awkwardness. We agreed to keep it private until we figure it out...or did he mean until he's tired of me. My mind trails back to the idea of how few relationships actually last.

I heard that his previous admin left because he was too demanding. Other than his weird habit of rarely looking directly at me, we work great together. People often use me as a go-between because I'm easier. Will that still be the case now that we've been intimate? Will I become the infamous 'last admin'?

This is all happening pretty fast, but I need to look out for myself. I could request a transfer to a different department if our work relationship gets uncomfortable. Hopefully, it won't come to that.

Until the road is clear, I'll take all the lessons I can get. My heart gets super comfortable again. Too comfortable. There will be fallout if this goes wrong.

I do the best I can getting ready without my normal hygiene products and makeup. Guess it's a casual day at work. At least my panties are dry. I don't have any video calls so I enjoy Lincoln's t-shirt, immersing myself in being his.

He made it very clear that I am...in the heat of passion. The dynamic of sex and power that strengthened me becomes a double-edged sword, and I'm the only one in this who doesn't know how to wield it.

I've made myself a spot on the couch when I see Jefferson walking back to the house. Diving into my work with more focus than necessary, I plan to use my power to keep from swooning at their feet every time they walk into a room.

Work during the workday. Play the rest of the time.

The front door opens and closes. He disappears into Lincoln's office, there's heated discussion but I can't make any of it out, then his footsteps return to the living room. He stops right next to me.

Okay, I was foolish. I can't pretend I didn't notice. A normal person would have acknowledged him entering. I'm not very good at this. I look up.

"Hey, how did your meeting go?"

"Really well." There's confidence in his words but it doesn't extend to his expression.

I tread cautiously. "I can take a break if you want to talk about it."

He sits next to me so I slide my laptop onto the side table.

Holding my hand between us, he leaves a tiny bit of space that sends volumes of warning. I brace myself mentally. I won't cry if he calls the whole thing off.

"I have something big to tell you. If it changes how you feel, I'll understand."

"Is this what you and Lincoln just argued about?"

"Indirectly. Before I tell you this thing...can I make love to you one more time?"

"Oh." Is this like getting a last meal before being executed? How bad can his news be? It's endearing that he didn't just offer a lesson then drop the bomb. I go with the only thing I can think of. "Are you married or something?"

"Nothing like that. I'm not a criminal or anything. It just might change the way you think about me, and whether you want a relationship." His eyes dart away.

A relationship? So, this is real, but how do I process information I don't have? The truth is that I love him the way he is, and if his secret makes him this nervous, I want to make love one more time with this version of him. After he tells me, I'll probably want to make love again because he trusted me.

"Lincoln knows?"

"Yeah, he was upset because I told him I wanted to make love to you alone."

"Oh!" Which must mean my boss is a little jealous. Interesting. Does he think this bit of info will cause me to turn Jefferson away, getting him out of the picture?

He cups my hand with both of his. "Baby Doll, I need you."

Sex isn't my specialty, but I am pretty good at talking to people. I forgo the ache between my legs and the tingles all over my skin at the thought of his body pressed to mine.

"Don't wait. Tell me now. I'm sure we can work it out if you trust me."

"You're young—"

"Give me a chance. I trusted you to teach me about sex and you said I was yours. Give me a chance to show you that you can trust me too."

He lets go, props his elbows on his knees, and drops his head in his hands. I wait patiently. He sits upright, turning to face me. "I've never been married. Never been in love...until now. I meant it when I said I love you."

Love? For real? Not in the heat of passion. Can I let my guard down? I open my mouth to return the sentiment but he cuts me off.

"Don't say it just because I did. Let me finish."

My palms sweat. Am I going to choose to walk away when I hear him out? My heart is patching the cracks as fast as they form, but if he drops a big enough bomb, will I run? I could beg my brothers to let me stay at their place.

Agony is etched in his expression. "Unfortunately, being in love isn't what it takes to make a baby...I have a ten-year-old son, Harrison."

"Oh..." I seriously need to broaden my vocabulary. "Okay." Not much better. I'm no math whiz, but that means his kid is only eleven years younger than me...how strange is that? Oh crap. Does that mean I have to choose Jefferson or Lincoln? Be an instant mom or a secret?

"I moved back to Eggplant Canyon to be near him."

"Wow, you're right. This is big. Can we go ahead and make love before I figure out what to do with that?"

His arms wrap around me. I've never felt so precious. Never felt so loved. His desperation to connect with me is tangible. We're a tangle of arms, clothes, bodies...until we're naked and joined on the sofa.

This time is different, slower and more deliberate, in contrast to the lust-filled session earlier. The weight of his body only partially rests on me, but it bonds us and connects us from our heads to our toes. Who could ever complain about Missionary? It's so intimate. His strokes are slow, giving me a chance to stretch around his thickness over and over again.

"I love you," I whisper into his ear.

His chest and his cock swell. "I love you too, Baby Doll. Don't leave me."

"I won't." I'm pretty sure I mean it.

His thrusts grow harder, his breaths more labored, and with each slide of his cock into me, my orgasm builds. My arms wrap around him, keeping me grounded as I spiral toward climax.

He grunts over me, his release filling my womb. "I want to give you babies, so bad."

I want that too. But my mind goes to Lincoln. I miss that he's not here with us. Angling my head toward the side, I see him standing at the edge of the living room. He's watching.

That's enough to let me surrender. The orgasm hits me so hard my world shatters. I'm blank. I'm bliss. I'm theirs.

Thirteen

Lincoln

Sitting at my desk, I can't hold a coherent thought. Everything takes me back to Natalie, my angel. How can we hide our relationship when we have to go back to work? Everyone will be able to tell I've fallen for her.

Is it too soon to ask her to quit and live with us? Would she even be willing to? Will we both get fired if word gets out? Jefferson was supposed to be here temporarily, but we could make it permanent. How would that work with his son?

My mind is in chaos.

How did sex lessons turn into love? Damn Jefferson for saying out loud that he loved her. She hasn't said it back, though.

Jefferson knocks on my open door and continues into my office, closing the door behind him. I'd expected details on his meeting with our neighbor lawyer who's helping him fight for custody. Instead, he hits me with wanting to have sex alone with Natalie in case she rejects him for having a kid.

Jealousy almost gets the best of me, but in the end, I want this to work with all three of us. It feels right. If we all want it, surely we can work out the complications. And it turns out I'd been wrong about Jefferson not fighting for his son years ago. He'd tried and lost, and it had been in his downward spiral that he'd taken up the devil-may-care attitude. All the more reason I should help him now.

I just don't want him to make love to Natalie without me there. It's a fair request though. We'll see if she agrees to it.

The computer screen dutifully shifts between emails as I click. Not a single word on the screen can hold my attention over the intimate sounds coming from the living room. He didn't even take her to bed.

Tension wracks my entire body. I need them. Stretching my neck from side to side fails to calm me. It's too much. I promised not to interfere, but I didn't say anything about watching.

Angel's moans are caught at a fever pitch. She's hanging on the edge of orgasm. Jefferson's large body on top of her petite one, her legs wrapped around his, and the sounds of sex as he slides through her tight pussy have my erection straining.

I'm a man of my word.

From the doorway, I watch, praying that if she can't deal with his news, she'll still give me a shot. Or would it be better to let her walk away from the *lessons*? I don't want to get her fired. Why so many damn rules in the workplace?

The fact that I couldn't work because I was thinking of my admin is one answer. The fact that I'm watching my brother's cock slide in and out of her as he ruts into my angel is another. They all point to distraction, but whether I work with her or not, that would be a problem.

I want to reach between them and circle her little nub with my fingers to help her clench the orgasm.

Their passionate whispers don't quite make it to my ears in a discernable fashion, excluding me from their moment. Jealousy boils hotter but I keep my distance.

I find peace in what I promised. I gave permission, as did she, apparently. The sensual tangle of lovers awakens the voyeur in me. And the fact that Jefferson and I are identical physically makes their carnal embrace fascinating at a whole new level.

She writhes and moans under him, so close to release. I want to see her face when she falls apart. What I don't expect is for her to open her eyes. Like she did with Jefferson when she was riding me earlier. She quickly finds me, and I swear, I'm the puzzle piece that helps her reach climax.

There's nothing like pure ecstasy on your lover's face. And I love watching my twin put it there.

The moment is serene. I should go back to my office so Jefferson can tell her the secret, now that he's had her in what may be his last time.

I honestly don't know what she'll say. He'd asked her last night if she wanted kids but detoured the conversation before she could ask him the same. Will her desire for children include a ten-year-old result of a broken condom?

My brother's head rests on the other side of hers, and she stares at me with half-lidded, sex-drunk eyes. He doesn't know I'm here. His intimate words are meant for her alone. "Thank you for convincing me to tell you before we did this. I love you, Baby Doll. We can be a happy family."

Her eyes fall shut. "I want that."

She already knows? He's always been the charmer. Always the one to take a risk and win. Did he plan it this way?

Competition and jealousy edge their way back to the surface. Am I a fool to think them letting me join them last night was anything more than a little fun while they're trapped in my house?

Fire burns through me. My hunger for Natalie is the problem. My involvement could cost Jefferson his son and Natalie her job.

Every dream about my angel goes up in smoke. The easy answer...the one that lets me protect my pride in the face of potential rejection...let her go...before they let me go.

My erection's long gone by the time they whisper a few more things I can't make out. I turn toward my office.

"Wait." Angel...Natalie's request is tempting, but I have to get my heart out of this.

I wave a hand over my shoulder. "I said I wouldn't interfere. I've gotta get back to work. We can fuck later."

Fourteen

Natalie

There are so many levels of uncharted territory, it's a relief to work the rest of the day. I think we all welcomed the chance to step back. Lincoln seemed to need space. Huge changes hang in limbo. Plus, my newly, non-virgin parts needed a little break. They got quite a workout.

When I'm on hold during a phone call, I browse the kitchen and set ingredients out for dinner. We'd snacked for lunch so this is the first meal I get to prepare. It gives me a cozy, useful, homey feel.

Lincoln hangs up from a call as he enters the kitchen and starts talking to me. He doesn't realize Muzak plays in my wireless earbuds. I disconnect my call.

"The road crews anticipate getting one lane open by tomorrow morning, and I've asked them to send a tow truck for my car. I'll have Jefferson drop me off at work. You can take the morning off to run home and get fresh clothes, and whatever you need to do. Or just take the whole day off."

Discomfort intertwines itself with my day.

"Thank you, but since I'll be heading into town to get home, I could drop you off."

"Jefferson owes me. It's fine."

"Okay." I motion to the items I've set out. "I'll have dinner ready at seven this evening."

"Thank you." His stilted answer and the distance he keeps between us intensify the change in demeanor I'd detected after he watched Jefferson and me have sex. My hands shake as I ask, "Are we okay?"

"Of course. You haven't done anything wrong."

"It just seemed like earlier, when you saw Jefferson and me, you didn't like that."

He shrugs, "Because I had to get back to work and couldn't fuck you right then? Or because you and Jefferson are turning sex lessons into discussions about kids?"

The sting pinpoints the problem. The solution remains elusive. Forcing the issue could bring heartache, but we have to talk.

I gently say, "It just happened. We didn't mean to—"

"Don't explain. I've never seen him happier. Having a woman by his side will help him look all the more stable while he tries to win back custody of his son. You can have a happy, instant family with him. I just hope you don't plan on quitting. It's hard to find a good admin."

He waves a couple of fingers as he turns and leaves.

I'm too stunned to form a question, and the one I need to ask is better suited for Jefferson. He said he came back to be closer to his kid, not that he had to win custody.

Has Jefferson taken advantage of me? Used the sex lessons to lure me into something bigger? Am I a pawn?

I shouldn't feel used and icky. I initiated the lessons. I shouldn't feel hollow.

The thing about sex and power being intertwined takes on a whole new meaning. I underestimated how much power I gave them when I didn't check my heart at the door.

But true to what's been said about men and sex, they're able to do it without emotional commitment. They're able to use it and walk away, which is exactly what I want to do right now...not from my job, just from this mess.

Anywhere is better than my boss's house. Needing breathing room, I toss enough clothes on so I can rush outside, thankful the storm passed. I call Nathan and leave a voicemail asking if I can stay at their place tonight. I'll clear my head then plead my case on their doorstep.

With no particular plan beyond that, I end up at the mudslide. Lincoln told us his car got stuck as the mud oozed around him, but with the storm and all of the lessons, I hadn't gotten outside to check it out.

It's staggering to stand at the edge of the muck where the side of the mountain simply sloughed off. Lincoln's lucky he didn't get hit by one of the trees or boulders.

Faced with the insanity of the situation, I call my best friend Zoe. Time to confess the mess I've gotten myself into. Maybe she'll have advice. When she doesn't answer, I head back.

"Hey," a woman's voice calls from the second-story deck of the nearby house. It's Madison Shepherd. She was a few years ahead of me in school so I remember her, but she doesn't remember me. It's nice to chit-chat and forget about my troubles until two men walk onto the deck and flank her rather intimately.

"Hey guys, meet Natalie, her brothers live two houses down and her boss lives in the next house. And Natalie, these guys are Jayce and Elijah...my boyfriends."

Plural? Maybe what I've done with Lincoln and Jefferson isn't as deviant as I thought. Not mainstream enough for us to pull it off while Jefferson fights for custody, I imagine.

On my walk back, voices from my siblings' rooftop draw my attention. They have a rooftop deck, and there's a half wall around it. All I can see are heads...three of them to be precise. One woman, who I recognize as my best friend Zoe, and two men—my brothers.

That's something I never wanted to see. I shudder and look away. What the heck is going on? Have I entered the twilight zone? Another threesome? No wonder she didn't answer. No wonder they didn't want me at their house.

I'd heard through friends that there was crazy stuff going on with the mayor's daughter and her three stepbrothers. I don't dare look across the lake to the mayor's house.

The walk leaves me with more questions than it answered. Diving back into work might be my only savior. I put my earbuds back in and call the company I'd hung up on as I make my way inside.

Fifteen

Jefferson

The second Lincoln ends the virtual meeting he's attending, I storm into his office. There's no tempering my anger, aside from not throwing a punch.

"What the fuck did you say to her?"

He spins around in his chair. "What do you mean?"

"What did you say to Natalie? Everything was perfect, then she was calling her brothers to see if she could stay at their place tonight."

"She got what she wanted from us, learned her lessons, and moved on." He swivels back toward his desk but I catch his chair back.

"No one walks away from what we have."

"Correction...Natalie does."

"Tell me what you said." I ball my fists while I tower over him.

He shoves me backward, and I'm about to go at him when he says, "I told her that you've never been happier. That she can have an instant family with you. And that I hoped she would stay on as my admin."

"But you're part of it. The three of us are a thing."

"Then why did you ask me to give you time alone with her?"

I would have felt the same way if our roles had been reversed. It's sibling rivalry at its worst. If I'm going to salvage this, I have to trust the two people I care most about.

"I was scared. I thought I was going to have to choose between my son and Natalie. I'd love to say there's not a choice, my son is my priority, but no other woman has nestled herself so perfectly in my heart."

"Or so you thought. Sorry dude. I told her to take the day off tomorrow because I don't know how I can face her in the office and not be consumed by how much I love her. How peaceful she looks when she sleeps. How sweet she is when she wants to learn something new. How giving her an orgasm is the most natural thing I've ever done...do I need to go on? I work with her. I can't date her."

"You fell for her too?" I consider that he never said it out loud like I did. It's not insane, but apparently the kid thing scared her off. Easier to agree to something in the heat of the moment than put in the work to own it.

"Do I need to take out a television ad? Yes, I fell for her...months before you ever saw her, and up until then, I had things under control. I don't want to be the asshole who gets to keep his job while the woman gets fired. I've seen it happen too many times. Plus, she's the best damn admin I've ever had, it's like she can read my mind."

"Like we've always done with each other."

"Yeah, sort of. Anyway, you said she's trying to find somewhere else to stay tonight? Maybe she's giving us the clean break."

I thought she'd come around to my kid, at least give it a try. "If my son freaked her out, I can't change that, but as far as a job, you could get a new job. You can work at my security company."

"It's not about the job. I can't have her working for anyone but me."

"You think you're protecting her? Some guy will steal her right out from under you if you don't make a move."

The door clicks open signaling that Natalie returned, so we silence our conversation.

Hope fills me when she appears in the doorway to my brother's office, even though her brow is furrowed and she worries her lower lip.

She points at her earbuds. "I'm on hold, but I wanted to let you know that after I get dinner ready, I'm going to bed early. The lessons were pretty exhausting...thank you. I should get some sleep."

She forces a smile.

I've been blown off by women, but it never made my soul hurt. I'm about to object when she motions to her earbud again, greets the person on the other end, and leaves us gutted.

Sixteen

Natalie

If there's a word that means agony but way worse, that's how I feel as I drive home. Lincoln and Jefferson must have left super early because there's no sign of them by the time I wake up.

The key is on the counter, so I lock up as I leave, and return it to where it was supposed to be hiding.

I could easily go home, get ready, and go to work. The only reason I'm taking the day off is that Lincoln told me to. He doesn't want me there. I'm now a risk.

Okay, he only said to take the day off... I put the reasons together.

Every ding of my phone has me on edge. I'm expecting HR to call or email and say I need to come in for a meeting. Lincoln's very calculating. It's only logical that he would get ahead of the potential disaster and spin it to protect himself.

Nonsense, Lincoln's not like that. He's so tender when we're not at work. Or was that Jefferson? They're hard to tell apart. If I hadn't been with both of them at the same time, I couldn't have even been sure I'd been intimate with both of them. It's just my broken heart panicking.

Broken heart? Am I so desperate for a relationship that I could fall in love in a day? Now I'm not being fair. I fell in love with Mister Adams long before.

Power cleaning my entire house and completing my entire beauty regimen, I try to keep my brain off Lincoln and Jefferson.

I'm not one to stand up for myself, but with them, I felt stronger, more worthy. I'd protected myself instead of believing that I could do more than "Be nice. Be pretty. Be useful."

If I can find someone to teach me lessons on how to grow beyond my mother's words, maybe I would be as fast of a learner as I was with sex.

But I've had enough lessons for a while. The next morning, I head into the office as if nothing happened. A definite sense of relief washes over me when no one makes a snide comment or looks at me funny.

Lincoln locked himself in his office.

Did I back out of our relationship just in time? Was it silly of me to think all of the sweet nothings that had been whispered meant something? I'm not sure I can handle working for a boss that avoids me.

Would it be better if I found another firm to work with? I pencil a note onto my calendar to make a decision in a week when I give this a chance to play out. I doubt he'll tell anyone about our secret affair. The question I'm going to answer in a week is if my heart can take it.

Will I still be second-guessing my decision to end things? There were too many unknowns happening too fast. I can't *what-if* every decision. The most important lesson I learned in all of this is that I need to be strong. That's one my mom hadn't thought of. She meant well with her mantras, and they worked for her, but they aren't me, and times have changed.

The phone rings, I answer, and my heart stops when it's someone from HR. I don't make out her name, just those two dreaded letters.

She says, "Oops, I think I read the wrong line on the phone list. Mister Adams asked me to call him directly. Are you his admin?"

"I am. I can put you through." What did I tell myself about him getting ahead of a potential disaster? Whatever tiny thread of my heart hadn't completely severed, has now snapped. Apparently, he *is* that kind of guy.

Be strong. Get ahead of things. No time like the present to start. I blurt out, "Before I do, I'd like to put in my resignation."

I'm met with silence.

"I'm supposed to notify HR, right?"

"Yes, but Mister Adams didn't say anything about you leaving too."

Too? He's leaving? Is he that worried I'll tell someone about our secret? I'm devastated. Tears threaten to spill. I let her know that I'll put her through to Lincoln, and as soon as I notify him through the intercom, I rush to the bathroom.

Lincoln

I spend the morning alone in my office, struggling with my decision. It wasn't supposed to be like this. We have some fun, we walk away with our secret, but the more I disconnect from Natalie, the worse I feel.

Knowing that she's five feet away from my office door, believing that I want anything other than to shout how much I love her is killing me. There's no way all she got out of the *lessons* was the physical act of sex.

I'd heard Jefferson's intimate words, *I love you, Baby Doll. We can be a happy family.*

Followed by her sincere reply, *I want that.*

It hurt that I wasn't included, but I can't let that be the reason I let her go. She's everything to me.

But words aren't enough, that's why I call HR and leave a message that I want to talk about my options for leaving. I note that they should call me back directly. If Natalie fields a call from them, she'll have every right to fear the worst.

As soon as I make a decision and implement it so that she'll believe I'm serious, I'll tell her.

I pace around my office, considering the corner windows, the heavy wood bookcases, and the overall luxury I've worked years to attain. If I quit, how many years will I have to put in at a new financial institution to gain it all back?

Raking my hands through my hair, I question the other option, and my sanity, to give it all up and take the job my brother offered. Having him as a boss stirs up the sibling rivalry, the constant comparisons, and never getting to be myself.

It was bad enough that we were always so equal and confusable. That had seemed like the worst. If I take the job, I'll be inferior, his employee.

But we could have Natalie.

With her in my life, I think I can handle the rest. And as much as Jefferson annoys me, there's comfort in knowing that if I ever can't be there for Natalie, he would be. She'd be cared for by the person I trust most in the world.

It's time to get over my ego.

Her voice comes through the intercom on my phone. "You have a call from Human Resources on line one...but you don't have to quit, Mister Adams, I will."

I'm objecting to her statement when I realize she's already put the call through. So much for HR respecting my privacy.

As tempting as it is to let Natalie quit since I'll lose my mind knowing she's working for anyone else, I'm the one with the standing job offer.

Reminding the HR rep about privacy, I tell her I'll have to call her back. Rushing out of my office, my heart sinks when Natalie's not at her desk.

Jefferson comes charging around the corner. "Lincoln, we have to talk."

"Do you know where Natalie is?" I ask.

"I assumed she was here with you."

We need a game plan. Ushering him into my office, I have to find out if he's as serious about her as I am. If he feels like a ship lost at sea without her? I'm not a boat guy, but the thought of drifting on the vast ocean with the horizon unobstructed on any side feels as hopeless.

"I'm miserable without her. I'm going to do whatever it takes to convince her that the lessons we can learn together are even better than sex. I need to know where you stand."

"Fuck, that's what I was coming to tell you. Fate brought us together and I'm not about to ignore the lessons Natalie taught me."

I'm put at ease that my twin and I are on the same page. It's like the universe is giving us the green light.

"Are you willing to let this be the three of us?" I ask.

"All or none."

"The judge might not look kindly on a relationship like this," I caution.

"I've gone over that possibility a million times, and we might have to lay low until I get custody back, but I'm trusting fate."

"If I take that job at your security company, do you promise not to lord it over me that you're my boss?"

"What do you mean?"

"I can't live without Natalie, and I don't want her to have to find a new job. If I work for you, will you be cool about being my boss?"

"You'd be my partner, my equal. That'll be easy. I'm more worried about convincing Natalie to accept me and my son."

I grab my cell phone and rush to the door. "You stay here. I'm going to find her. If she shows up, call me."

When I find her in the Human Resources office, she tries to excuse herself, but I catch her arm. "Come with me."

"I didn't say anything," she whispers as I guide her into the hallway.

"I trust you."

One of the HR reps calls out, pointing out that this isn't a good look. I take my hand off of Natalie's arm and nod for her to come with me, which calms the rep down.

"Then what are you doing?" I ask. Safely away from prying ears, I add, "Don't quit until you hear Jefferson and me out."

"I get it, we had fun, but I know this isn't real. I heard his call."

I struggle to keep my voice down, to do anything but wrap her in my arms and kiss her. "First of all, the lessons you taught me are the biggest dose of reality ever. And second...which call?"

The wind deflates from my sales as I admit confusion.

"When he told his lawyer he could look like a family man now."

"We better get back to my office. He's there. We can explain everything."

Unable to touch her as we navigate our way back, my hands shake with the need to hold her. When we're close, intimate, I can sense every emotion she has, and right now, I desperately need to know that she feels loved.

Jefferson rushes to her as I pause to lock the door. When I turn around, I'm frustrated to see that she's motioned for him to stay a step back.

This conversation can't happen fast enough. I offer her a chair, but she stays by the door. We give the distance she insists on. We're like hungry wolves surrounding our prey, and I catch the flicker of nervousness in her expression before she ducks her head.

I nod at Jefferson and he takes a step back when I do. With the breathing room, she lifts her gaze appreciatively.

Seventeen

Jefferson

Seeing my baby doll flinch away from us hurts me at levels I didn't know were possible.

Lincoln leads. "Jefferson, Natalie overheard a call where you made her feel like you were using her to keep up appearances."

My hands fly up, reaching for her, but she retreats into the door.

"This is hard enough. I won't be used. What we had was fun, and I'm ever thankful that you were both so generous to teach me, but I don't owe you anything. And I can't confuse your son about my role in your life. I can't confuse myself."

Her words grow quiet with the last statement.

"There's nothing to be confused about. We love you. We want you to be ours."

She shifts her eyes from me to Lincoln. "You do?"

Lincoln reaches for her hand and she lets him take it so I do the same with her other.

He says, "Our lessons have only started. There are so many more. Please, Natalie, be the one to teach them to us."

"I'm the one who needed lessons, not you."

Lincoln says, "We gave you lessons about sex, but you gave me lessons about cherishing what's most important in my life, about the risks I'm willing to take, and what I'm willing to give up."

"But you love your job. I felt horrible when I heard you were quitting."

I jump in. "He's going to be my partner. We're going to run the security business together. That means you can stay here...but you don't have to work if you don't want to."

Her eyes go wide. "What would I do all day if I don't work?"

"When we're home...we'd appreciate it if you let us love on you. When we're not home, you can do whatever you want."

"Just preferably not around any other guys," Lincoln adds.

Her brow furrows. "You don't trust me?"

"I do..." Lincoln looks at me and I nod. "We do. You just make us insanely possessive. If we could permanently close Eggplant Canyon and live alone with you, we would."

"Aside from the obvious problems that presents, I'm flattered."

I have no doubt she'll be an amazing mother to my son, I can feel it in my soul, but I make sure she's thought about it.

"And to clear up what you heard me say on the phone...I'd been ahead of myself. I'd love for you to meet my son because even though I've been a terrible dad, it's my priority to be an active part of his life. Are you willing to take on the role of a stepmom?"

Her mouth drops open. "Um...are...you asking me..."

My pulse pounds in my ears while we all process what I just asked. In a really crappy way, I proposed to her. I've never wanted to be married, never wanted a woman in my life permanently.

Lincoln saves me. "Marriage is tricky with three people...and by tricky I mean not possible, legally, but in every other way, we're prepared to fully commit to you."

"I have an unsupervised meeting with my son this afternoon. Will you please be there?"

"It's all happening so fast."

"Is it? I've been in love with you since the first day you stood in this doorway and told me you were going to be my new admin."

"The first day?"

"Yes ma'am. You wore a light pink dress that matched the blush of your cheeks. The little white sweater you had over it made me want to wrap my arms around you and keep you warm, and I suspected that if I did, I'd never want to let you go."

"But you hardly ever looked at me. I thought you hated me."

"I didn't want to scare you with how badly I wanted you."

"What would you have done with me?" Her sultry tone changes the direction of the conversation. My cock springs to attention.

"I would have broken our company's fraternization policy on the first day. That's how sure I was that I wanted you."

"It was the same way for me, Natalie. The moment I saw you snooping around on Lincoln's porch, I wanted you. So how about it, can I introduce you to my son?"

Eighteen

Natalie

"Can we all three be there?" I ask nervously. My life was calm and calculated until coming to work for Mister Adams. My world has changed. My perspective has changed. I've been loved, and I'm no longer going to deny it.

"I wouldn't have it any other way."

"Yay!" She wiggles her fists in the air. "I've always wanted to be a mom...but I won't be overwhelming. I'll give him time to warm up to me."

Jefferson comforts me. "You're going to make a great mom. It's in your nature. What would you say about us trying to make you a mom right now, in case we didn't already do it?"

"Have you been spying on my search history?"

The guys laugh. "No, why?"

"Because I looked up how to remove an IUD. The internet said it's possible to just pull it out."

Lincoln lights up, his controlled demeanor giving way to pure excitement. "And we could knock you up today?"

"I don't know if it can happen that fast, but I'd love to try." I'm all smiles and nerves and excitement.

Jefferson moves beside me and walks me to Lincoln's desk. "Have a seat, Lincoln."

They do their twin thing of looking at each other and understanding what's being said without words.

Jefferson positions me across from Lincoln, stands behind me, and lifts my dress. The warmth of his hand sliding over my ass sends shots of electricity through me. We're way past breaking corporate policy, but since Lincoln and I are both quitting, we don't have much to lose.

Lincoln leans forward in his chair, steepling his fingers in front of his mouth. "Are you about to get bent over my desk and railed?"

"It seems that way, Mister Adams."

Jefferson slides my thong down and I step out of it. I'd had a fantasy about doing this with Lincoln, but with him *and* his brother, I can barely breathe.

Lincoln wiggles a finger for me to lean closer, and I prepare for a kiss, which he gives me, but only briefly before he reaches for my top.

"If I'm going to concede that Jefferson gets to be the first one to fuck you in my office, I'm going to enjoy the show."

Thrusting my chest out, I rub my breasts on Lincoln's hands while he tries to maneuver my buttons. By the sounds of it, Jefferson's stripping down behind me.

"Natalie…" Lincoln cautions.

"Yes, Mister Adams."

"If you don't behave, I'm going to rip your dress open."

"But then I wouldn't have anything to wear."

"All you need to wear is our cum."

I laugh. "To walk out of here?"

"If we do it right, you won't be able to walk. I'll carry you out."

"That could be embarrassing." I quit wiggling so he can get the front of my dress unbuttoned.

Jefferson helps me get my arms out then slides the fabric down my body. Lincoln makes quick work of my bra. It's a lot of hands and activity, but we mesh like we read each other's minds. Like we're made for each other.

Jefferson flattens a hand on my back and nudges against the outsides of my ankles to get me to put my feet close together. "Keep quiet, Baby Doll or your boss will have to reprimand you."

Lincoln had been kissing me and pulls away for a second to wink. "Be a good girl and make your boss happy."

Jefferson's fingers dig into my hips and his tip presses at my very soaked entrance. I want to make a quippy comeback but my mouth falls open as my sex stretches around Jefferson's thick, hot cock.

Lincoln catches my gasp with a deep kiss, his tongue fucking me the way his twin is taking me from behind. We fall into a rhythm and soon, fingers toy with my nipples, hands massage my breasts, I'm surrounded by love, the verb, and love, the noun.

My body becomes theirs. My orgasm winds inside of me tighter and bigger than I've ever experienced. Then my mouth is free and lonely, and I fall forward slightly at the loss.

It gives me a second to remember we didn't pull out my IUD. If I wasn't so full of Jefferson, I'd be disappointed, but that emotion isn't possible when I'm barreling toward release.

My boss sits back, looking so fucking stately in his big, fancy office chair. He runs a hand over his slacks that barely contain his straining cock. His eyes are on my tits, as promised. The hint of a grin rounds out his confident style. He's pleased, and that makes my sex tighten. He teases a thumb over my lips, making my walls tighten even more.

I won't make it much longer. Jefferson's groans match my urgency.

"Need something to suck on, Angel?" Lincoln asks.

I take his thumb into my mouth but lose suction with a giant slurp and pop sound. Jefferson's cock swells.

Scrambling, I reach with my tongue, sucking him back in. His eyelids fall shut on a stuttered breath. "You're so beautiful, Angel. Clamp down on his cock and come for me."

From deep inside Jefferson, a groan rumbles through the room, shaking my body, offering the last touch I need to unravel. I suck hard on Lincoln's finger, channeling my moans and cries into the effort, holding my eyes open to watch the sheer pleasure that takes over his expression.

I'll never close my eyes during sex again...except for when bliss overtakes me.

In the last second before my mind swirls into euphoria, I'm aware of the sharp thrusts of Jefferson's hips against my ass. The warmth of his seed coating my insides. And his whispers as I drift away. "I love you so much, Baby Doll."

My next coherent moment is Jefferson's cock sliding out of me. Lincoln's standing, withdrawing his finger out of my mouth, and bends to kiss me on the top of my head.

They switch places.

When Lincoln's behind me, he says, "What was that you were saying about getting rid of your birth control?"

"It's possible to pull it out. That's all a doctor does."

"Will it hurt you?"

"It shouldn't."

"Then let's get rid of this thing because I'm not playing around about wanting to get you pregnant."

Nineteen

Jefferson

Standing beside my lawyer, I acknowledge the judge's declaration that he has come to a decision. I haven't been this nervous since a few weeks ago when Lincoln walked Natalie into his office and I didn't know if she would accept a life with us.

Okay, that's not a long time ago, but these are back-to-back the two times I've been most nervous in my life. I'll take it in exchange for the amazingness of everything I love coming together.

Commotion behind me catches my attention. My son wedges himself between Lincoln and Natalie. That has to play in our favor. He adores her, and she loves taking on the role of mom, in the short spurts we've been allowed to get to know him.

And she's already pregnant, but we haven't told anyone yet. The three of us agreed to publicly downplay our romantic involvement until I get custody, but even if that happens in the next few minutes, we'll hold out a little longer. No courtroom PDAs.

I wish I could be sitting with them, holding their hands, bracing for the decision. It's not the same—even the few feet of separation with them in the front row—but I'll be away from them briefly to secure a future with my whole family.

My son's mom isn't a bad person, she's just not convinced I'm ready for the role. I'm determined to make it as seamless as possible because my son deserves nothing but the best. Thankfully his mom did a damn good job of raising him when I wasn't able to get my shit together and step up to be a dad.

Rubbing my sweaty palms on my slacks, I take calculated breaths to keep from passing out. I watch the judge's mouth move. His words enter my ears. He said equal custody. My brain replays his words over and over, securing that I heard him correctly.

Then I spin around, hop over the wooden partition that separates me from my family, and gather them in a hug.

We planned to take Harrison on a picnic at the park closest to the courthouse whether I was granted custody or not. Now that I live in Eggplant Canyon, I'm only twenty minutes from his mom's house and we'll be doing a lot more playdates and family time.

Officially having custody of my son is validating at a level I didn't remotely understand. Hearing him squeal as Natalie explains that he gets to spend half of his time at our house swells my chest to the point I think I might explode. Apparently, love

Natalie

It's been a long day and couldn't have worked out any better. My brothers are outside at their house when we get home. I texted them as soon as we got the good news, but the icing on the cake is that my best friend is there too.

Accepting that my best friend and my brothers were a thing stirred up all of my cringe factors, but Nathan and Carson had just as much trouble accepting that I was in a threesome with my boss and his twin. Zoe and I had a big talk that ended with us deciding we're pretty darn lucky to each get two wonderful guys.

And now I officially have a son.

They head over to congratulate us, and our ménage doesn't seem as strange when we're with like-minded company. Not everyone understands how we make it work, but in Eggplant Canyon, it's becoming the norm. The only hold-out is Jefferson's lawyer. Time will tell if there's really something in the air up here or if it's purely chance.

Epilogue

Natalie

All of the neighborhood moms are corralling their kids to the lake for the first group swim lesson. Madison, Aria, Calli, and Yvette have joined Zoe in being my best friends. Turns out that whatever's in the air in Eggplant Canyon finally got to the lawyer, but that's a different story.

With enough kids to make you think Eggplant Canyon needs our own elementary school, we hired three swim teachers to come to our little lake. Our husbands insisted that we hire female instructors, claiming that women make better teachers, but watching each of the three buff, college guys strip off their tank tops and play with our kids, I have no doubt we made the right choice.

Not only do we get to enjoy the scenery, but we also get a break, the kids learn an excellent skill, and even though the mudslide is long gone, we live in our little bubble of happiness where no one judges us for our relationship choices.

Halfway through the lessons, Lincoln's car rounds the corner. Jefferson is with him. They're supposed to be meeting with the local motorcycle club to talk about hiring a bunch of the bikers to expand the security company.

They stop near us and Lincoln rolls his window down. "Get in the car, Natalie."

The irritation in his tone concerns me. Did the meeting not go well?

I tell the other moms I'll be back in a minute. It's great to have support, and know that they'll watch my kids like their own, but I'm worried about what's upsetting my husbands.

Jefferson's out of the car, holding the back door open for me. He ushers me in and sits beside me without explanation. The heat spilling off the two of them has a weird vibe to it now that I'm close to them.

"What the hell is going on?" Lincoln asks as he hits the gas.

"Swim lessons. I put it on the calendar."

"What happened to the instructors?"

Oh, so that's what this is about. I suppress a smile. "What do you mean? Ashley, Kelly, and Chris are doing a great job with the kids."

Lincoln parks in our garage and whips his head around. "Ashley, Kelly, and Chris are guys?"

Sinfully hot, muscled, tanned guys, but I better leave this as a simple, "Yes."

"We told you to hire women," Jefferson says.

"You did, but when the other moms and I had to make the final selections, this is who we ended up with." I taunt them with a shrug and slide out of the car. "How did your meeting go?"

"Not so fast, Baby Doll." Jefferson catches my hand, spins me around, and pins me to the wall of the garage. He presses the button on the wall so the door closes. "Out of all of the swim teachers, you ended up with those three?"

It tickles me that my guys are jealous, and based on the size of their erections tenting their pants, they're insanely worked up. It's a little crazy though. They have to know I'm completely smitten and satisfied with them. We have sex every day.

Sometimes one of them entertains the kids, other times we wait until the kids are all out of the house or in bed so the three of us can be together.

Lincoln presses close to us, grabbing my chin and turning me to face him. He traps my mouth with a kiss and lowers his hand to the apex of my thighs.

"You better not be wet," he grumbles through our kisses. As if they read each other's minds, Jefferson is inching my skirt up.

"Why not?" I play innocent. When I first hooked up with them, I was, and while I still look the part, there's no question that I'm far from it.

"You better not be hiring those young boys to come around so you can fantasize about them."

"You think I have time for that?"

"Tell the truth." Jefferson nuzzles his lips on my ear.

"How can I be anything but drenched when the two of you are sporting erections and have me pinned against the wall?"

Lincoln tucks his fingers inside my panties and my insides knot in anticipation. I'm left wanting though when he pulls his hand away.

Drawing it up between us, he says to Jefferson, "You see that?"

"Looks wet to me, bro." Jefferson grabs his brother's hand and pulls it under his nose. "Yeah, she's definitely been thinking about fucking."

The two of them shake their heads, adopting a playfulness that tells me this is going to end very well. Lincoln unfastens his belt and I expect him to drop his pants, but he grips my wrists and wraps them with the leather.

I feel a little guilty that I'm not watching our kids' first swim lesson, but I'm not about to break this up. He threads the belt tightly, turns me to face the wall, and lifts my hands, securing them on one of our coat hooks.

"You disobeyed us, Angel."

"You're not the boss of me." I can't say it without a chuckle. I peek under my arm. The two of them are stripping down. I may have thought we'd tried every position imaginable, but this is a new one, and the orgasm tightening inside of me is already considering it a winner.

Jefferson strips my panties then gathers my skirt around my waist.

"I may not be your boss anymore, but if you're busy ogling younger guys, you won't be getting this cock." His shaft is so hard when he slaps it against my butt cheek, I question whether it was really him.

"Good thing your twin can take your place." I angle myself toward his brother.

"Fuck." Jefferson mutters. "Sorry dude, you dug that hole for yourself."

He slides his tip inside of me. His insanely rigid heat tells me we've struck on yet a new way to keep our relationship fun. A little bit of jealousy seems to go a long way.

By the time he's stroked me into a frenzy, Lincoln's begging for a turn and fills me with his equally hard and hot shaft. I'm surrounded with and filled by love as they swap back and forth, giving me orgasm after orgasm until they finally can't take it any longer and fill me with plenty of seed to make a third baby.

If we're lucky, our neighborhood will have one more kid in nine months.

And we live happily ever after!

A bonus scene for this story is available exclusively to newsletter subscribers. With plenty of friends/babysitters in the neighborhood, Natalie, Lincoln, and Jefferson schedule a kid-free stay-cation every year on the anniversary of the mudslide. Grab this bonus scene for a fun little guessing game of who's who and see if Natalie can tell them apart!

Sign up at: https://SylvieHaas.com And true to my initials, SHhhh, I'll let it be our little secret.

Claimed by my Best Friend's Brothers

A Ménage Romance
Part of the Eggplant Canyon series

Sylvie Haas

Blurb

I've had a crush on my best friend's older brothers for as long as I can remember...long before they made a fortune designing high-end homes, and their success puts them even further out of my league.

Being the bratty friend of their little sister never gave me much appeal. Dropping out of college and working, temporarily, as a maid doesn't exactly sweeten the deal either.

Or does it?

When opportunity presents itself, will I risk losing my best friend by cozying up to her brothers?

If you love dirty-talking men who have over-the-top ideas of how to please their woman and want to give her babies, these guys are ready to snuggle up with you in the middle!

One

Nathan

My knuckles whiten on the steering wheel as I make the final turn into Eggplant Canyon. Why is there a car parked at our house?

My roommate, Carson, is also my half-brother and business partner. We cut the single day of vacation we planned off the end of our business trip when the client asked if we could cut two weeks off the end of the remaining four weeks of the project.

I'm not in the mood to deal with whoever owns the older model, convertible BMW.

"You expecting someone?" I ask Carson.

He looks up from his phone, furrowing his brow at me before following my gaze. "We're not supposed to be home, why would I be expecting anyone?"

"Thought you might have invited a friend over to help blow off some steam."

"All we do is work. Which friend would that be?"

"I'll assume that's rhetorical. The more immediate question is why someone thinks they can park in our driveway?"

I scan the upper and lower decks, not seeing anyone. Surely our meticulous neighbor, Lincoln, would have noticed. He likes things tidy, thus he's aware of everyone's comings and goings, but it's the middle of the day so he's probably at work.

Pulling between the thick columns in front of our garage, I park next to the intruder and note the car's faded paint job that's more of a gray than the original silver offered on that model.

Not a car that would have escaped our neighbor's attention.

"Could it be the maid?" I wonder out loud.

"I scheduled her for the day after we left," Carson confirms what I already knew.

We get out of the car and while I retrieve our bags from the trunk, Carson checks behind the house.

"There's no one here," he says from the corner.

With only six houses in the canyon, we all watch out for anything suspicious, but some neighbors are more attentive than others. The lawyer three doors down is second most likely to take notice since he's into details, but I glance at his house and there's no sign that he's home.

Carson loosens his tie and slides it from his collar before unbuttoning the top couple of buttons and yanking the bottom of his shirt out of his slacks.

"Here are my few seconds of fun in the sun before we buckle down and deal with our new deadline. I was tempted to tell the homeowners to go fuck themselves," he grumbles as we head for the front door.

"If designing this house wasn't guaranteed exposure in Engineering Marvels Digest, I would have beat you to it. The waterfall feature in the master bedroom is too hard to pass up." I slide the house key into the lock and the soft scent of coconut catches my attention. Not like actual coconut but a fragrance.

"You smell that?"

Carson's gaze narrows. "Yeah, where's it coming from?"

We glance around but the owner of the car, who I'm assuming must be a woman, is nowhere to be seen. The light breeze must have carried the scent. There's something intoxicating about it, beyond simple coconut, but it's gone with the wind's shift.

I unlock the front door and step inside.

"I'm going to grab a shower before we get—" Carson crashes into my back when I come to an abrupt halt.

Stepping to the side, I motion to the large purse on the kitchen table. A woman. Okay. This can't be good. I call out, "Who's here?"

Carson raises a brow when we're met with silence. "Suppose Goldilocks took a liking to one of our beds?" A grin breaks out on his face. "I call dibs if she chose mine."

The moment of humor doesn't diminish the fact that somebody broke into our house and is still here. Was it a break-in? The door was locked and doesn't appear to be tampered with.

"Sight unseen? Are you that desperate?" Continuing inside, we close the door and call out again. Still no answer.

"It's been a while, but fair enough...I call the first right of refusal." He knocks on the door to the bathroom then peers inside. No one.

The open concept floor plan flanked almost entirely with windows to maximize the views of the mountains, leaves no doubt we're alone on the first floor.

Carson follows me upstairs. Better not be a damn Goldilocks sleeping in my bed, although if she's the tropical treat I smelled outside, I might change my mind.

A surprising pang of disappointment hits when I find my bed empty. A distraction is the exact opposite of what I need right now. I step back into the hallway at the same time as Carson who meets me with a shrug. We check our shared office next and I pick up a delicate scent, not only of coconut but something seductively sweet. If this woman looks half as good as she smells, I'm going to lose the battle with my threatening boner.

The windows in each room allow us to check the second-level decks as we continue our search.

"Goldilocks must have gone for the rooftop deck." Carson leads up the interior stairs to the roof.

"Someone up here?" he calls out while swinging the door open.

We freeze as we step out. For the first time ever, the sight on our deck is more captivating than the view of the mountains. And coconut mixed with the feminine scent from my office has become my new favorite scent.

Goldilocks is stretched out on one of our deck chairs. Her expanse of golden-brown skin is marred only by a tiny white bikini that barely contains all the parts it's designed to cover. Her face is turned away and her long brown hair gently floats in the breeze. Her arms extend overhead, one hand resting on the other.

I tamp down the desire to pin her hands in place, straddle her, and shove my cock down her throat. The insane thought serves as a reminder that I should start making an effort to date.

Goldie's younger than us by around ten years, a rough estimate I make as I continue my fantasy with thoughts of sliding my dick into her tight pussy. Fuck.

"Dibs. Definitely dibs," Carson says as we continue staring.

"I bought the chairs she's on, which gives me first right of dibs," I only half joke.

"Whatever, but I'm liking your idea about blowing off some steam before we get to work." Carson approaches and calls to her again, "Hey."

Not to be left behind, I keep pace, and as we stop a few feet away, the subtle sounds of rock and roll drift from her wireless earbuds. The peaceful rise and fall of her breasts indicate sleep. What the fuck is going on?

"I guess we need to wake her up," I whisper to Carson. The problem is that I want to do it for all the wrong reasons. I want to know if she's the kind of girl who considers getting her ass slapped a good thing. I want to hear my name on her lips as she comes on my cock.

"Uh, yeah." Carson makes no effort to quiet his voice. "And after she tells us how she ended up on our roof, we can find out which bed she prefers."

Shit. My brain already forgave her for breaking in, or whatever she did. Carson's been as consumed with work as I have. We both need a break.

Sunlight glistens on the luscious mounds of her breasts that threaten to fall out of her bikini top with each breath. I nudge my elbow into Carson's arm. "That's not a bathing suit, is it?"

"I think she's in her bra and panties."

"And sunglasses," I add as I make a half-hearted effort to maintain a shred of decency. With all of her bare skin, it takes a second to convince my cock this is *not* an opportunity. The wild craving I have to change her divinely flat belly into a swollen one carrying my child is complete nonsense. Maybe we should have kept that vacation day on the schedule. I'm getting delusional.

"We better do this before she wakes up and thinks we're perving."

It's understood that we're both desperate to drag our fingers through the sheen of perspiration on her skin. Matching each other inch for inch, we each extend a hand, tapping her elbow, so closely we might as well be one.

She startles to life. We jerk back and give her a second. Her arms pull down, her hands covering her chest. There's an almost imperceptible pause before her head turns our direction.

A shriek is the only hint of her voice as she sits up, her legs spreading on either side of the chair as she rips out her earbuds.

Damn if my eyes don't drop to her barely covered pussy spread for us. The sudden awareness that she's neatly shaved is not helping my uncomfortable situation any.

The moment is fleeting though. She tosses her leg to the far side of the chair, stands, and faces us, one arm across her chest, the other barely covering more than the scrap of fabric between her thighs. I clench my fists to keep from reaching for her.

"What are you doing here?" Her head turns to Carson then lands decidedly back on me.

"We live here," I say while Carson shrugs off his already unbuttoned shirt and hands it to her.

"Put this on."

Jealousy courses through me as she does what she's told while her head swivels with three double-takes of Carson's bare chest. Damn him. Is it really that crazy to think her compliance is anything other than her not wanting to be underdressed near strangers?

She looks good in the oversized shirt that she's clutching closed in front of her chest. Too good. My cock strains against my pants.

"You, Nathan Moore, live here with Carson?" She pulls her sunglasses down to peer over them then shoves them back in place with a scarlet red manicured fingernail. Her bright blue eyes stir a familiarity inside of me. Do I know her? Am I so obsessed with our business that I could forget a woman like her?

I step closer but my shins hit the chair. "How do you know my name?"

Her jaw inches to the side as she worries her plump lower lip. Carson adds other relevant questions before she has a chance to answer.

"You mind telling us who you are and how you got into our house? And where your clothes are?" His tone is demanding but soft as he adjusts his slacks.

When she lifts her hands as if begging for a moment to explain, the shirt falls open.

I get another glimpse of the tiny white panties I'd love to rip off so I could put a baby in her flat, bare belly. My work-to-play ratio needs serious adjusting. What the hell is wrong with me? It's not like I've never seen a beautiful woman. The familiarity of her eyes haunts me.

"I'm sorry. I can explain."

Does she catch my gaze and the tension in my jaw as I struggle to understand why I'm about to lose my mind over her? Or maybe she notices my shameless cock. I can't tell because of her sunglasses. She clamps the shirt closed with one hand, leaving the other extended outward. Reasonable that she's holding us at bay.

She probably thinks I'm going to devour her. I take a deep breath and glance at Carson. He's as bad off as me. We're decent guys but she doesn't know that. Or maybe she does.

I take a deep breath. "We're not going to hurt you, but we do need answers, like how you know my name."

Yeah, I'm hung up on how this insanely gorgeous woman knows my name.

"You're Natalie's older brother." She pauses, giving me a second to let her enchanting voice release its stranglehold on my balls.

Connecting her to my younger sister of eight years isn't helping. I haven't seen any of her friends in years, and none of them looked like Goldilocks.

"And you're…" I lead her to elaborate.

"Zoe Simon."

I choke on her name. My little sister's best friend? Impossible. I watched her grow up. My pulse accelerates. I have to force my eyes not to travel down her body again.

"Take your sunglasses off."

She dips her head, removing them with the hand that's holding her ear buds, then lifts her gaze. My dick gets no reprieve when she obeys me without question.

126

The breeze whips her hair across her face and she fusses to tuck it behind her ear as her brilliant blue eyes bore into my soul.

Fuck. Carson and I stare, speechless.

I've never met anyone with eyes as intense as hers. As a teen, she'd outlined them with thick black makeup, died her hair black, and rarely made eye contact. Other than being surprised my sister hung out with a girl as weird as her, I never gave her any thought.

My sister would kill me if she knew what I currently wanted to do to her best friend.

"I'm the maid. That's how I got in. Carson Yeager was the owner's name listed on the cleaning ticket." She shifts her focus to Carson.

"That's me, Natalie and Nathan's half-brother, although we hardly ever saw each other growing up. But the maid was supposed to be here a few days ago."

She worries her lower lip again. "I'm filling in because the regular girl quit. Please don't tell my boss. I just got back to town and if I get in trouble, it could cost me more than my job. I'll finish cleaning and get out of your way."

"Hang on, Goldilocks, that doesn't explain where your clothes went." Carson pulls us back to the intriguing question.

She has to have clothes. There's no way I'll get any work done if my little sister's best friend is parading around with this much gorgeous skin showing. How have I not seen pictures of Zoe? Guess I should keep up with my sister more.

Two

Goldilocks

"What?" Did he call me Goldilocks or is the heat getting to me? Or am I still lost in sexual fluster over Nathan seeing me practically naked? I've played out countless fantasies of him, but this is much more nerve-wracking. I attempt to hide my unease. "I can't be Goldilocks, I don't even have blonde hair."

"You're practically naked on my rooftop deck, begging me not to get you fired. I think I can call you whatever I want," Carson says.

I should be worried about what could happen given my predicament. Instead, the nickname makes my sex tingle and I suppose there's an element of comfort that Carson is Nathan and Natalie's brother. She only ever mentioned him a few times since he lived really far away.

"I should get dressed." That is going to be difficult since my clothes are in the washing machine.

"Don't do it on my account. I'm just wondering where your clothes went," Carson feeds the wanton excitement brewing inside of me.

I search his expression for a hint of humor. There's none.

He's serious? My gaze flits to Nathan. Our eyes lock briefly, his jaw flexes, then he hurriedly looks away as he rakes a hand through his hair.

Natalie would kill me if she knew her brothers had just caught me in my underwear and bra, and liked it. She hated being the younger sister to a heartthrob. Girls of all ages tried to befriend her, or in the case of some of the older ones, they wanted to babysit her to get closer to Nathan. If Carson hadn't lived so far away, he'd have doubled the trouble.

I kept my attraction to him to myself, which was made easier when he moved out since he's so much older.

I glance around. The half-wall around the rooftop deck minimizes my exposure.

"I spilled coffee on the way here. The schedule said you weren't getting home until tomorrow, so I didn't think it would be a problem to put my clothes in the washer."

"Fine. Maybe you should do up a few buttons, though," Nathan adds, looking everywhere but at me.

"Maybe?" The question slips softly through my lips before I can stop it. Years of pent-up frustration take their toll.

"Button the shirt." Nathan's forceful tone sends exhilaration through me. Are there other things he'd like to command me to do? Well, since he's telling me to button the shirt, maybe not. But I saw the way he and Carson looked at me. Even if nothing comes of it, he doesn't completely see me as the little sister anymore.

With my head bowed, I slowly button my way up, carefully maneuvering the hand that's full of my stuff. Am I crazy to feel something...for both of them? Guys like them probably want a woman who makes something of herself, and a woman with experience.

After being a good daughter, starting the engineering degree, and doing the internship my dad arranged, I quit college, fully convinced that listening to my parents had led me down the wrong path. A desk job would be too confining. I like freedom and ideas. But because my parents controlled most of my life, other than graciously allowing me to go through my goth phase as they'd termed it, I've been kind of lost.

Little did they know, they were the reason for my goth phase. A small rebellion.

I'm practically a stranger to myself.

My goal for the next couple of years is to make enough money to get by and figure out what Zoe Simon wants to do with her life. I need to break the habit of being dependent on people to make decisions for me.

Since my parents left town, moving back to Peach Bottom Valley provided an element of safety. And my new boss, Skylar, who I've known for years, offered a couch and a job until I get my feet on the ground.

"Stop." Carson's gravelly demand pulls me from my thoughts.

I glance at him then quickly back at my hands. I'm about to fasten the button that's even with my breasts.

Whatever *Zoe* is going to do with her future may be uncertain, but if *Goldilocks* is reading the room, or rooftop correctly, the attraction isn't just one-sided.

Can I take notes from the fairy tale? Beg for forgiveness rather than ask for permission... Is it different if I'm begging forgiveness for screwing my best friend's brothers who also happen to be my employer's client? Yeah, that's not cool.

I could have a little fun with Carson since Natalie barely considered him her brother. Just a little. Nothing that would piss Natalie off or get me fired.

Is that how you like it? A little cleavage showing? The words are on the tip of my tongue and that's where they need to stay.

The heavy silence doesn't stop the fantasy from playing out in my mind.

I like it when you obey. Carson's voice would crack a little. His possessive tone, despite the hitch, would hit me hard enough I could barely breathe.

Looking up at him from under my lashes, I would cleverly parry, *"I like it when you tell me what to do."*

Even if a solar flare made a direct hit on this roof, it would have nothing on the heat between us.

The sun must be getting to me. Is there such a thing as a heat fantasy?

"Come here." Carson would demand.

Wait. He really did. The fantasy world vanishes, leaving me to make a real-life decision.

Nathan clears his throat and shifts. I meet his eyes. They're different, darker. What I'm feeling is real. If I had to choose between the two guys, the only reason Nathan would be my second pick is his closeness to Natalie.

I give myself a mental shake. My job. The couch my boss is letting me sleep on. My best friend. This is insane. Until I finish bartender classes and get a job doing that, it's time to shut this mess down.

Slightly egged on by my daylight fantasy, I say, "Thanks for the shirt, and the buttoning advice. I better finish cleaning."

Rounding the end of the lounge chair, I keep a wide berth.

The corded muscles of Carson's neck flex and his hand extends toward me, falling short as if rethinking his decision.

Be a good girl and do what you're told. Hints of Carson's husky voice blow through my mind as the fantasy resurfaces.

Now I have another reason to save up money and get over my fears of living on my own. I need an intimate session with my vibrator, which I won't be getting on Skylar's couch. My college roommate worked nights so I had plenty of free time to "deal with things".

Perhaps because my fantasy has made my legs weak, or because my body has turned traitorous, I stumble. Carson catches my waist and my arm.

If there was any doubt about the weak legs and traitorous body, my lack of movement delivers the answer. Carson's grip is firm and perfectly matches the way his gaze has caused me to soak my underwear. It's also a perfect pairing for the sexy banter I so desperately want to draw from him.

The back of his hand trails up my arm, which is frustratingly covered by his giant shirt. It's a momentary disappointment though as he continues over my shoulder, up my neck, then unfolds his fingers to cup my jaw.

"You okay, Goldie?"

I nod, forcing myself not to look at Nathan. It's bad enough that I'm certain he can tell how badly I want his brother.

Carson's hand grips my neck and his lips part. Or maybe I'm having another heat fantasy?

I'm melting into him when suddenly we're thrust apart. Nathan shoves a hand on Carson's chest, causing him to let go of me.

The heat of Nathan's body on one side of me and Carson's on the other grants my unstated wish. Is there a world where I don't have to choose?

Nathan's arm briefly grazes my breast as he separates us. He pulls it back like he's been burned.

"Hey neighbors," someone's words faintly pass through my mind and I'm in a whirlwind of confusion.

Who is that? We're on the roof.

The weight of denial, or is it rejection, burdens my chest.

"Oh, sorry, did I interrupt?" A man's voice calls from next door. The houses aren't crammed together, but they're not exactly far apart. As I look over the half-wall, I easily see the neighbor standing on his balcony.

"Fuck off, Lincoln," Carson says and takes my hand to lead me to the other side of the deck where the neighbor can't see us.

The magic is broken.

"That's weird, Lincoln's not usually so relaxed," Carson says.

Nathan's shaking his head. "This is wrong. You're here to clean. Put your clothes on as soon as they're dry, and leave as soon as you're finished."

As we take the stairs into the house, I question if I'm foolish to hope we can recapture the moment. Since I was raised to do what I'm told, I'll finish cleaning then leave.

Three

Carson

"So what if she's our little sister's friend. Lots of people have live-in help." I keep my voice down even though Nathan and I are in the living room while Goldie finishes cleaning upstairs. Nathan's not keen on my idea to hire her for more than once a week cleaning.

"Our little sister's *best* friend, and I know her." Nathan drops his head into his hands, his elbows firmly planted on his knees.

"Noted, but you didn't even recognize her."

Nathan flops against the back of the couch. The poor guy's in agony. "She didn't used to look like that."

"We could use help these next two weeks. Cooking, cleaning, errands, and whatever—"

"Fine. Let's call Skylar's Good Maids and find someone else, though."

I clasp my hands behind my head. "Has to be her. If it makes you feel better, I'll foot the whole bill."

"Money's not the issue. I know you want to fuck her."

"You're jealous that I consider her fair game." I'd almost nutted in my pants when she stumbled on the deck and I'd caught her. Then when Nathan and I had her pinned between us, a primal need to claim her took over.

"Don't let this come between us." Nathan's in a tight spot, but we're all adults.

"Dude, she's not off-limits just because she knows Natalie."

"Yeah, she is."

"According to you. Let's let Goldilocks choose."

"What?"

"See if she'd rather be our maid or our..." I raise my eyebrows.

Nathan drags his hands down his face then pounds a fist into the couch cushion. His eyes are closed as he shakes his head. "Only the maid part, not the rest."

Nathan insists that we focus on how we're going to regroup our workload with the revised, two-week shorter, schedule.

We hash it out until footsteps coming down the stairs catch our attention.

Goldie's bare legs come into view, and my cock's hard again. When we first came inside, we offered her a pair of sweats but everything we had swallowed her petite frame. I flop a throw pillow onto my lap to keep from looking over-eager.

Nathan does the same. I stifle a laugh. Poor dude.

The sway of her hips causes me to sort out my conversation with Nathan. Did I say I wouldn't pursue her? Not exactly.

She pauses between the two of us. "My clothes will be dry in five minutes. Is there anything else you need me to do?"

Get down on your knees and suck my cock. I keep that to myself.

Nathan forces a smile and shrugs. The silence is ripe with sexual tension.

Her crystal blue eyes move between us and her hands are clasped in front of her pussy. She wants to make us happy, I can see it. I can feel it. I also don't want to be a jerk to my brother.

Then I open my mouth, my voice low. "Did you do everything you were supposed to?"

Why am I such a mother-fucking asshole that I have to imagine her taking my orders? She nods, but the look in her eyes is my real answer. I've tapped into something.

Nathan cockblocks. "Here's the deal." He exhales hard before continuing. "As you know, we were supposed to be home tomorrow. We're designing this ultra-cool house and were out of town talking to the homeowner and builder. Turns out they want to start construction sooner and asked us to cut two weeks off our timeline. It's almost impossible unless we have help."

If he's only asking her about the maid service, this setup isn't necessary.

His voice lowers and he adds, "You know Natalie would kill me if anything happened between us..."

Goldie nods. "Yeah, she hated the way girls threw themselves at you, especially when they were nice to her to get to you."

Does the light in her eyes dim? Damnit, Nathan. I shoot him a glare, which he ignores.

She looks at me, a hint of something mischievous in her eyes, and my smile flickers back to life. My mind's a hotbed for wild thoughts.

Nathan rambles on...a definite sign he's uncomfortable. He needs a sense of control. "We're *not* looking for a relationship, and we're not going to be good company, but would you be willing to be a live-in housekeeper? Cook, clean, and run errands. We'll pay of course."

So clear. So disappointing. So exactly what it will take to keep him from shutting the whole thing down.

Confusion crosses her expression. "Live here?"

"We'd give you the spare bedroom upstairs, between ours," I add. Not the way I'd like her to be between us, but it's a start. Nathan's optional in that scenario of course.

Four

Nathan

Knowing there's only the tiniest scrap of fabric keeping Natalie from being exposed, I barely keep my eyes off her bare legs. It shouldn't matter that she's wearing Carson's shirt. It doesn't mean anything. Nothing. And I am fully capable of not thinking of her sexually.

Or so I wish. I force my brain back to the details of our proposition. I mean job offer. Fuck me.

"It's a work arrangement. There's plenty for you to do. Let me make that perfectly clear. You're Natalie's best friend and I don't want to cause any trouble. You can hang out and sunbathe. Aren't you in college? Are you free for a longer commitment?"

I'm not sure when I started pacing. Is my sweating obvious? I wipe a hand across my brow and force myself to shut up.

I don't know if it's the idea that Carson might pursue her that has me flustered, or if it's how badly I want her but don't want to cross a weird line. There's no way this is a good idea. Surely Zoe sees that. She was always a smart kid.

She giggles. That sound could undo me.

"I dropped out of college. Need to sort a few things out."

"What were you studying?" Carson asks as if having a conversation with someone as gorgeous and not dressed enough as her could be normal.

She waves the comment off. "What my parents told me to. Anyway, I just got back into town. Everything I have fits in my car. A friend is letting me crash at her place, so honestly, living here for a couple of weeks would be great. I can save up money for my own place and give my friend a break."

"What?" I choke on what appears to be her agreeing to stay here. We need rules. First, she has to wear pants. Mine. No, not mine. Hers. Shit.

"Is it okay if I keep the other cleaning jobs Skylar gave me? Nothing too time-consuming. I can still do everything you need."

Disaster loading...

Carson manages to answer. "I don't see why not."

Zoe balls her fists and taps them together in front of her chest. The gesture accidentally pulls the shirt up. The extra inch of thigh accelerates my heart. What am I, a fucking Victorian? Excited by ankles. This is definitely not her ankle.

"Great. I'm scheduled to do a few of the houses in Eggplant Canyon so I won't have to go far."

Why is that comforting? I need her far away or I'll break into a full sweat.

"And I always wondered what it would be like to live on the jizz."

Carson and I simultaneously lose our composure. Our coughing and choking sounds cause Zoe to reconsider her statement.

Her hands fly to her mouth. "Oh my gosh. I assumed you knew that...in high school, everyone called the little Eggplant Canyon lake the jizz?"

Neither of us speaks.

She twirls her hand as if we're supposed to be able to catch up. "You know, because of the shape of the big lake...and this little lake looks like...seriously, you've never heard that?"

Her cheeks are bright red. It wasn't lost on me that she avoided stating what the peninsula looks like. I would pay to hear "cock" muttered from her sweet lips. I'd pay even more to have my...nope! Abrupt halt.

I'm grateful Carson jumps in. "I can see why. Count on high schoolers to think of that."

I'd graduated eight years before Zoe and Natalie, so it must have come up after my time.

"Come to think of it, I didn't hear it until my junior year. Guess I assumed the little lake had always had the nickname."

She may be the one blushing, but I can't take more of this. I'm too tempted.

"Yeah, well, thanks for the education."

Carson's cracking up. "These next few weeks could be interesting."

Yes, they will. And somehow, we have to finish designing and engineering the house for our client while all I can think about is letting Goldilocks try out our beds.

Five

Zoe

Curling up on my super-plush bed, I stare out the giant window at the brilliant sunset erupting behind the mountain.

This is a dream come true. Living in the jizz.

I squeeze my thighs together at the meaning I'd like that to have. I'm just a college drop-out, biding her time as a maid, though. Any interest I thought I saw from them had to be part of my heat fantasies. Plus, Natalie would kill me.

I flop onto my side and pull the pillow onto my face. Not like I have a chance. Nathan probably still thinks of me as a little girl. He seemed so uncomfortable offering me the job. Like he was trying to talk me out of it.

Now I get why Natalie never showed me a picture of Carson. How can she be so lucky to have the hottest brothers on the planet? Maybe that's not lucky.

I do a mini-scream, not wanting either of the guys to hear.

Natalie's parents made it clear that her brother made a name for himself as an architect for unique, high-end homes, and I'd heard about their half-brother, the engineer, but I'd never dug deeper.

Avoiding asking about Nathan or searching him up on the internet had been the only way to keep my crush on him at bay.

At least I can benefit from his success for two weeks. Then back to my real life.

I jump up, slide the glass door open, and sprawl onto a deck chair. Live it up while I can. This is way better than Skylar's couch in Peach Bottom Valley. The houses are scrunched together, allowing the maximum number of middle-classers to live in the cozy mountain town.

I can't judge though... At least she has her own house.

With what the guys have agreed to pay me on top of the money I'll make from the other cleaning jobs, I'll pad my savings and have time to ponder my future while living the high life. These two weeks will be my encouragement to get a high-paying job so I can keep living like this.

The buzz of my phone brings me back to reality.

Natalie: *Are you settling in?*

I need to break my arrangement to her gently.

Me: *Skylar hooked me up with some great clients.*

Those damn dots come and go from the screen. I fire off a quick message before she has a chance to send a judgy comment telling me I should go back to college. Ugh, if I didn't love her...

Me: *in Eggplant Canyon*

Natalie: *Zoe...*

If only I didn't want so much more, with either of them, or both of them. If I wasn't moving in, this would be so much less awkward.

Me: *I cleaned your brothers' house today*

Natalie: *Don't let them be jerks*

Me: *they seem pretty cool*

Natalie: *you're destined for a lot more than picking up after my brothers*

I knew she'd say it. Cooking and cleaning in exchange for great pay and getting to live here isn't a bad trade-off. I'd stay longer. I'll save the full story for a rainy day, which we're about to have a few of. There's a big storm coming.

I'm just not sure how I'll deal with my sexual frustration. They work from home, so I won't have much time alone. And with my bedroom sandwiched between theirs, I have two walls that might betray the buzz of my vibrator.

I'll figure it out. Two weeks can't be that bad, can it?

Six

Carson

Uncurling my fingers from my unbearably hard cock, I grumble a curse at myself for not being able to stop the dirty train of thoughts that all feature Zoe.

Our housekeeper.

Our little sister's friend, blah, blah, blah.

I don't care who she is. If I can't get some sleep and get my head straight, I'll never be able to meet this accelerated deadline.

This is no less than the third time tonight I've woken up fucking my hand. I stroke my thumb over the pre-cum that's insisting I deal with my one-track mind.

Nathan's probably doing the same thing. There was no missing the way he looked at her. We spend so much time working we haven't had to worry about being attracted to the same girl.

In the interest of common decency, I try to derail thoughts of Zoe. My spank bank comes up blank. Good. Maybe I can get some sleep.

I punch my pillow into shape and sprawl across my bed.

Neither Nathan nor I have gone on more than a handful of dates while we've been building our empire, our reputation, and our future. When our style of home design became the hottest thing on the market, and there seemed to be no upper limit to what people would pay to have us as their design team, we made a pact to capitalize on it.

We devote our lives to making a shit-ton of money while we're en vogue. That's how our million-dollar mountain home is paid off and we have healthy retirement accounts in place.

Next thing I know, I'm waking up with my cock in hand again. This time, I don't resist.

I'm wound so tight, I might not even need lube. Every thought of Zoe shuttles me closer to release. That scrap of panties that barely covered her pussy. Her breasts spilling over the top of her bra. Even her smile and the way her eager, light blue eyes overflowed with happiness at the prospect of working with us.

Knowing that she's in the next room is almost more than I can handle. Nathan's right, keeping our relationship with her strictly business is the only way we'll get through the next two weeks.

If we end up fighting over a girl, a woman, a goddess... It won't end well personally or professionally.

My cock throbs at the thought... A faint buzzing catches my attention.

With a slow drag of my hand over my cock, I stall my craving enough to focus on the sound. I assumed it was from outside, and would pass, but it's not growing any closer or farther like a vehicle would.

The cyclic hum is coming from Zoe's room.

Shit. I shuffle upright, resting against the headboard. My dick's standing at attention, straining thicker than ever, as I stare at the wall across the room.

If x-ray vision was real, I'm certain I'd be watching Zoe waste an orgasm on a dildo. She should never have to please herself. I'll take one for the team. She can lie back and let me do all the work.

Pre-cum spills down my shaft. I wrap my fingers around it, rotating my hand to spread the slick seed. How wet is she? How sweet is she? I tamp down a growl.

Am I just a pervert who assumes she's getting herself off in the middle of the night? What else could it be?

Oh, what I'd give to find out if she's flat on her back, sliding the lucky silicone through her tightness. Or does she have a suction-cup style so she can sink herself onto it the way I'm imagining her straddling me, taking my length an inch at a time—slowly while she stretches to accommodate me, the rosy beaded nipples of her tits giving me a distraction while I give her time.

When she's fully seated on me, I'd wrap my hands around her waist and pump her up and down, cherishing the bounce of her tits while her walls clamp around me.

"Ohh." A muffled moan is quickly silenced. The cyclic hum switches to a steady, quieter sound. Any belief that she was doing anything other than getting herself off is shattered.

My release hits so hard and fast, I shoot all over myself before I can reach for a tissue. These hot streams of cum would look so much better on her silky belly with me towering over her. She'd be wearing nothing but pleasure and my mark while she looks at me with her sinfully gorgeous blue eyes.

Barely audible moans come through the wall.

Shuffling sounds from her room draw me back to reality where my heavy breaths are the only other sound intruding on the silence. Jesus Christ, I'd heard her come. Had she heard me?

Climaxing at the same time as Zoe could be my life mission.

The wall separating us has to go.

How am I supposed to deal with her having to take care of herself? Is it arrogant to think that she was wishing it was one of us?

I have two weeks to find out.

Seven

Nathan

Waking up to the aroma of bacon with a hint of something warm and sweet, maybe pancakes, fills me with happy memories—of times when I was a kid and had people around me who loved me. No chance it's Carson doing the cooking.

Zoe wraps my heart around her little finger a little bit tighter. She's always been kind and smart, but now that she's grown up, her inner beauty radiates with an allure I've never experienced. A torturous seduction when combined with her womanly curves. A forbidden fruit.

I roll myself out of bed before I replay any more images from the moments before I knew the woman on my rooftop was off-limits.

Throwing on sweats and a t-shirt, I head downstairs. She has her back to me. Her short shorts and tank top give me a stiff reminder of why I kept dreaming of her. My mind hadn't played up her beauty. Every bit of what taunted me in my sleep is standing in front of the stove.

Long tanned legs, brown wavy hair, curves highlighted by her form-fitting pajamas... We might need more ground rules than which tasks she's responsible for. Better coverage from her clothing would give me a chance to regroup. My brain is racked with the desire to walk up behind her, slip my hands around her waist, and plant a kiss on her neck.

She turns, catching me staring before I'm able to divert my gaze or act casual.

I toss out, "Smells delicious. I could get used to having you around."

That would have sounded better if I'd stopped before the last comment.

She giggles and I'm reminded of how cock-stroking the sound is.

"Just pancakes and bacon. I'll get your plate ready." She motions for me to go to the table.

"I can do that."

"You guys are paying me really well. Let me take care of you." Her smile is genuine and does all the wrong things to me. When she stands beside me to set my plate down, I have to close my eyes and breathe. Focus on the bacon.

It's part of the arrangement that she'll cook. Simple. Got it. She's doing her job.

"Are you going to eat?" I ask.

"In a minute."

I wasn't prepared for how it would feel to have her serve me. That wasn't part of the deal, but not an illogical extension either. Domestic. Like we have a relationship. Like she's a part of my life.

She's our housekeeper for two weeks, nothing more. The reminder does nothing for the extra tug of tightness she has on my heart.

This arrangement is such a bad idea. I agonize over the right thing to do. If thanking her and swatting her ass weren't on the forefront of my brain, I might be able to say something.

"Hey there," Carson's voice eliminates any chance I had of reeling myself in and clarifying that our relationship is strictly business despite my ability to control myself.

I grumble a greeting in return.

"Good morning," Zoe says and returns to the counter. "Have a seat. I'll bring your plate."

"I'll say. Best morning I've had in a long time." Carson's tone hints at more than a good night's sleep or appreciation of having breakfast made. I'll chalk it up to the obvious...her damn shorts that give the slightest glimpse of the curve of her ass cheek. The perfect place for tucking a hand to pull her close.

"I'm glad you slept good," she says.

"Actually, I didn't sleep that great. Woke up a bunch..."

Why does Carson let his words trail off instead of explaining why waking up would lead to the best morning he's had in a long time? I hadn't noted sarcasm.

The glass bottle of maple syrup falls from Zoe's hand, clattering against the plate.

"Oh no. I'm sorry. That's probably too much syrup." She scrambles to clean up.

Carson crosses the kitchen, stopping extremely close beside Zoe.

Distance buddy. Remember our agreement. Or is it too late, did he already cross a line? Is that the tension I'm sensing? No, he's way too chill for anything to have happened.

"I can handle it. Won't be too sweet for me." He reaches around her.

I slump with a sigh and an eye roll at his cheesy line. Perhaps he needs a reminder that she's only twenty-one. She'd be in college if she hadn't dropped out. We haven't considered college girls as dating prospects in a few years. She's our employee. So many reasons to be careful.

He carries both of their plates to the table. The dynamic of our house has completely changed. Is it just that she's a woman? That I'm attracted to her? That I can't have her?

"Have trouble sleeping last night?" Carson asks Zoe. There's more to his question.

Zoe studies her pancakes as she cuts them. "I might have woken up a few times. Probably just getting used to a new environment. The room is great, the bed was super comfortable."

"As long as you were comfortable. I thought I heard you at one point."

Zoe freezes.

What the hell is going on?

She stammers. "Um...yeah...sorry if I woke you up."

"I wouldn't mind if you did... If you need help with something, getting comfortable, or whatever."

"Thanks."

"Just knock on my door. Call my name. You may be taking care of us, but we're not opposed to taking care of you too."

Shit. That's a suggestive way to term our arrangement, but the vibe they're giving off tells me they're talking about something else.

We manage to get through breakfast without either of them revealing what happened. I won't embarrass Zoe by asking in front of her.

When she finishes her food and leaves the room to start a load of laundry, I keep my voice down. "What the hell was that all about?"

Carson grins, and I curse that valuable time is being lost with his evasiveness.

I lean closer. "You better not have done anything."

"She got herself off in the middle of the night."

Jealousy courses through me. "How the hell do you know that? Did you walk in on her?"

"That would be a sight." Carson shoves his empty plate away and sits back. "I'm not that lucky. I heard her through the wall."

"You're serious?"

He nods.

I watch the entrance to the laundry room even though I can hear that she's still busy. "How can you be sure?"

"She uses a vibrator and her moan... That pool of maple syrup she drenched my pancakes in has nothing on that sweet sound."

"She's off-limits."

He mumbles something that doesn't sound like agreement.

Dropping my head into my hands, I accept that we've made a horrible decision. Carson and I will have such bad cases of blue balls, we're going to be worthless.

I raise my head.

How can he be so calm, almost happy?

I'm tense enough for both of us. I clarify, "Through the wall, that's it, you didn't go to her room when you heard her..."

He shakes his head. "No. I gave you my word."

I nod. "Thanks."

"I just don't know if I can keep it."

Eight

Zoe

The rich scent of a cigar comforts me when I enter Carson and Nathan's office. Curiosity over which guy is the cigar smoker is settled when I see a candle burning. Interesting.

I'd avoided the guys after breakfast, unsure how to handle Carson's basic admission that he heard me masturbating. The immediate embarrassment had quickly given way to exhilaration.

Living with two hot guys takes a toll on a girl. I've never experienced so much attraction, to the point I had to give myself an orgasm in the middle of the night. The way Carson brought it up shocked me at first, but I think he liked hearing me. Is it naughty to be glad I gave him a show?

Will he tell Nathan? The poor guy seemed to be in the dark.

I step to the candle, using my hand to waft the fragrance to my nose. The label reads, *Cigar Lounge*. "That's a surprisingly realistic scent."

Carson laughs and it occurs to me that both men are watching me instead of doing their work. He says, "It's a win-win. Cigars smell great but I'm not of fan of all the health problems, and my hands are usually too busy to hold a cigar anyway."

Nathan adds, "Yeah, and it's cool that candle makers realized guys like to burn candles too but don't necessarily want a pink or purple candle with floral scents. Although, I saw one called *Grease Monkey*, and I wasn't sold on the automotive scent. My days of having to work on my own cars made that a scent of necessity not a scent of fun."

"Hmm... Maybe I should swap my perfume for Eau de Whiskey," I tease.

Is that a growl that I hear from Carson? Is he irritated I'm interrupting their workday? They made it clear that their timeframe to get the project wrapped up is really short.

"Sorry, I won't disturb you. Just came in to round up the trash."

"No problem. But you better not suggest things like bathing yourself in whiskey when I'm supposed to be working." The strain in Carson's voice is intoxicating.

Nathan wastes no time detouring his brother. "We should get back at it. Check your email for the new idea I want to pitch to our clients. I don't know what I'll do if they don't like this concept."

I'm bummed their attention returns to their computers. Their attention bolsters me. Like we mesh, and I'm better when I'm around them.

Which is decidedly an overzealous way of acknowledging I appreciate them hiring me. It goes back to my life-path assessment. I'm good at obeying and making people happy. My temporary status as a maid fills that in an unexpected way.

Getting back to work, I empty Carson's trash can. While I'm at his desk, I notice the blueprint that's pulled up on his computer. It takes me back to my brief college stint.

I cringe at the thought of being tied to a desk every day...unless they tied me to it. Oh geez. I shake the thought.

Anything that requires a primary focus on computer screens or paper sounds like the tolling of death bells. Thus my failure to complete the engineering degree my parents insisted would be good for my future.

I chuckle that this probably isn't what my parents had in mind when they envisioned me working with engineers. I step to the other side of the room to Nathan's desk. Technically, he's an architect, so I guess I'm only working with one engineer, or if you consider the pair, a design team.

They never once took into account what I was good at or what I wanted to do. They've run my entire life for me, leaving me dependent on other people to make my decisions. I dump the nearly empty trash can into the bag I'm collecting trash in. If I had a clue what I wanted to do, I could have switched majors in college, but the more I looked into my options, the more it became clear I need to learn who I am.

In a frustrating life assessment, the only thing I could confirm I'm good at is doing what I'm told and pleasing other people. I have big ideas but no execution.

I pause, peering over Nathan's shoulder. He has computer renderings of a bedroom on his screen. A waterfall on one of the walls... I like it.

He glances over his shoulder. "Everything okay?"

I point at the screen and smile. "Yeah, sorry. I like that waterfall."

"Hopefully the clients will." He rubs his head.

Instinctively setting a hand on his shoulder to comfort him, I'm surprised by the connection, the jolt of electricity that shoots through me, and the sexy bulk of his muscles.

It hadn't escaped me how well he filled out his dress shirt or his t-shirt, but actually touching it, I'm taken by the mass that's bigger than my hand. My sex tingles and although I'm not experiencing a heat fantasy, I imagine myself straddling his lap.

If he told me to do it, I'd follow his command and make him happy even if Carson was watching. That's a surprising thought.

SmorgasSmut, the local social media gossip site, has been spreading rumors of ménages in Eggplant Canyon. Has it gotten to me?

Geez, what's wrong with me? I finish what I need to do in their office and leave.

Taking the trash can out to the street, I pause a minute to breathe in the clean mountain air that smells of rain.

This side of the ridge, although only four miles away as the crow flies, is a world apart. The neighborhood is nestled in the canyon, tucked away from the rest of the world. Peace, tranquility, and—

"I don't believe we've met?" A deep voice breaks through the serenity.

I spin toward the man, the neighbor, who's striding from his house toward me. It's sort of a relief to talk to someone I don't work for, and have a dangerous attraction to—not that the neighbor is unattractive.

"Hi. I just moved in. I'm Zoe, Nathan and Carson's housekeeper."

He raises an eyebrow. "Housekeeper, okay, I'm Jefferson Adams. I just moved here too, into my brother's place."

"Oh, you're Lincoln's brother. I'm with Skylar's Good Maids. I'm scheduled to clean your house tomorrow."

"You really are their maid?"

My mouth falls open as I catch his assumption. I hold both of my hands up between us. "Yes. For now. I qu...took a break from college, and I'm working while I regroup."

"Nothing wrong with hard work. Speaking of... Do you know Madison, she's about your age, moved back in over there?" Jefferson motions to the end house.

I went to school with Madison, but we weren't exactly friends. She had a social life and was popular, unlike me.

Talking with Jefferson makes me feel like part of the neighborhood like I'm really moving in. A portion of my fear of living alone is put to rest with how easy it can be to meet neighbors.

I make a mental note that when I buy my first house, I'll look for a good neighborhood. More likely, an apartment. That would give me lots of neighbors.

Most people would probably find that crazy, but being on my own scares me. There's always the possibility that holding a job and making money will help build my confidence.

Jefferson says, "The financial institution my brother works at has a lot of great savings options, and bankers who love helping young people learn the best ways to put their money to work. I can give you a business card when you come by tomorrow—"

"Zoe, we need you inside." Carson's voice is stern. Am I in trouble? My heart sinks that I might have messed something up on my first full day. I turn and am shocked by how quickly he's crossing the clearing between the houses.

He's glaring at Jefferson. Carson's fingers wrapping around my upper arm are the only indication that he understands I'm present. His jaw is tight, and his fingers grip tighter than I would consider casual. It's possessive, similar to the way he said he needed me inside. I glance between Carson and Jefferson.

It is possession. And I like it. A lot.

I step closer to him. My body fits so naturally against his. He moves his arm around my shoulders. My pulse pounds so hard in my ears, I lose track of what the men are saying.

Jefferson's eyes shift to Carson's hand on my shoulder.

Shit. What am I doing? Will Jefferson get the wrong impression? That my maid services are more than traditional cleaning? Oh god, I hope I don't get fired over this. Any efforts to be independent and learn to live on my own are undermined by the comfort of Carson's embrace.

"Just meeting the person who's supposed to clean our house tomorrow."

"She cleans your house and that's it."

"Whatever, but be careful about what you do on the rooftop if you want to pretend she's just a housekeeper."

"Nothing happened up there." Carson's fingers dig into my shoulder. That shouldn't send a bolt of excitement to my sex, should it?

The tension between the two of them arguing is lessened by snuggling into Carson's side.

He's just protecting me.

Jefferson rubs a hand over his mouth and turns to me. "I'm not judging. And just to be clear, I don't expect any special services."

Carson doesn't respond. Just keeps a firm grip on me as he guides me home.

Natalie barely knows Carson. She'll have to cut me some slack.

This may only last two weeks, but I'm going to enjoy every minute of it.

Nine

Zoe

The doorbell rings and I stuff my cleaning rag into the plantation blinds to mark where I left off.

"I got it," I call out as I climb down the ladder so the guys don't have to stop working. They may not have even heard the bell since their office door is shut and rock and roll is playing fairly loudly. It's been a few hours since Carson blew up at the neighbor. He's avoided me ever since.

If I wasn't supposed to talk to the neighbor, he should have told me. No need to get pissy. The only communication we've had is Carson texting me not to worry about dinner.

I see the bouquet of flowers before I get to the door. Red roses. Not the kind of bouquet friends or family send each other. How had I not even thought about the guys having girlfriends? Natalie always talks about Nathan being a workaholic with no social life and I guess I assumed Carson was the same way.

That doesn't mesh with his breakfast comments or the way his arm wrapped around me, which I can still feel. The security he'd enveloped me in had been more intense than I'd ever dreamed another person could provide.

All for not. All the better reason to learn not to need people. When I get my own place, there will be no mistake who the flowers are for when the delivery guy shows up.

Opening the door, irritation wells in my throat that I'll have to present one of the guys, most likely Carson, with flowers from his lover. Damn it.

"I've got a delivery for Zoe Simon." He looks at me expectantly, and for a little longer than should be necessary since that's me, but I'm dumbfounded.

"Are you Zoe?" he asks.

I nod. "Um, yeah. These are for me?"

"They sure are." He hands the vase to me and takes off, clearly not as intrigued by the moment as I am. Is Natalie being funny, sending me flowers for putting up with her brothers? No, she shouldn't expect me to be back until next week.

The distant rumble of a car catches my attention. This secluded neighborhood doesn't get much traffic. Two cars at one time is practically a traffic jam.

Closing the door, I take the flowers to the kitchen table and admire them. It takes that long for me to process the wonderful scent.

I pluck the card from the foliage. It reads:

I'm sorry.

Carson

Sorry? For what? There's another knock on the door. My head whips to the side. A pizza guy, based on the flat box he's holding.

I return to the door. Did he tell me not to cook because he ordered pizza? I would have made one if he'd asked. There are a lot of things in my life that I don't have figured out, but I'm a good cook. My parents had insisted on it. Cooking is a great people-pleasing skill.

Despite all of my frustration with my parents, they did what they thought was right. But if I'm being honest, culinary skills are a positive aspect of my upbringing. Many of my friends can barely boil water.

"Hang on, let me get my wallet for a tip," I tell the delivery guy. Then it dawns on me that I don't know if I should have tipped the flower deliverer. Too late.

"It's okay, there was a generous tip left online. Thanks." He leaves and I'm left with the box warming my arms and the scent of tomato sauce, herbs, and yeasty crust filling the air.

I hate to take it to the table and adulterate the scent of the roses. If we had different circumstances, I'd think an apology, roses, and a pizza would indicate a date.

The music from upstairs shuts off and their office door clicks open before footsteps trail down the stairs. With the weirdness of the conversation with the neighbor and subsequent apology, is it presumptuous to assume I'm invited to eat the pizza?

The guys head downstairs and Carson bee-lines for me, giving brief attention to the bouquet. He takes the box and heads to the table. "So, you got the roses. Are we okay about this afternoon?"

I follow him to the table and Nathan is behind us. I continue to get plates and napkins.

"We're okay but I don't understand what you're sorry for."

Carson ducks his head and glances at Nathan, who nods. Carson rolls his shoulders. "I'm sorry for scaring you. I didn't know Jefferson had moved in. He has a reputation and it...I didn't want you getting caught up in anything."

"You didn't scare me." I grimace. "It was tense and a little uncomfortable, but you made me feel safe." Did that come out wrong or just as I wanted it to?

The corded muscles of his neck flex. Nathan fidgets in his chair.

"I'll always keep you safe."

"Thank you. I know that being a maid can't seem like much to successful guys like you, but this is huge for me. And your generous pay, while giving me a place to sleep, lets me save money a lot faster. I can't screw this up. If I don't live up to your expectations, please tell me." My breaths are shallow. I want Carson and Nathan to protect me and tell me what to do. I want their praise.

"You're doing a great job, and we love having you around."

He's soothing my worry about being alone. It's natural for him. He can protect, I can nurture. Where does that leave Nathan?

Hungry, apparently. He flips the box open. "We're happy to help. Better eat it while it's hot."

The mood shifts. In between all of my insecurities and fantasies, these guys are some of the easiest people to be around. We get each other.

And when I roll my neck to each side, Carson notices.

"Your neck hurt?" His eyes hold too much sincerity and interest for this to be a simple question.

"Mostly my shoulders." Then I recall stuffing the rag in the blinds. I never finished cleaning them. I point to the ladder. "I was dusting the blinds when the deliveries came. Sorry, I didn't realize it was time for a break."

I get up to retrieve it, but Carson catches my hand. "Don't worry about it. Why don't we watch a movie? I can give you a shoulder rub."

There's almost nothing on the planet that sounds better than Carson's hands on my body. I look at Nathan and ask, "Is that okay?"

"We're all adults." He holds his hands up, moving them back and forth a little too enthusiastically. "Who am I to say no?"

I'm not sure if a massage will relax me or get me worked up, but I'm willing to find out. It lays the foundation for considering a relationship with him once our work arrangement is over.

"What do you want to watch?" Carson asks.

"Anything." It's true. The chance I'm going to pay attention to the screen is zero.

"You must have a favorite," Nathan says.

"I'm always singing the praises of Pride and Prejudice, but we can pick something the two of you would like also."

Nathan laughs. "You and my sister."

I love Natalie dearly, but I'd rather not think of her when I'm with her brother.

He regroups as if he's also frustrated that he brought her up. "I've seen it. I love it. The architecture is gorgeous."

"I'm game to watch. Whatever makes you happy. I appreciate you saying you weren't scared when I blew up at Jefferson earlier, but I saw how big your eyes got. You froze." Carson chucks a finger under my chin. "You can be honest with me. And we're going to watch your favorite movie while I give you a massage so I can make it up to you. No disagreement allowed."

"Okay, thanks," I say sheepishly. I can't be honest with him. That would require me telling him that what he overheard last night was me fantasizing about him and Nathan claiming me while I rode my vibrator.

Carson sits against one end of the couch, dropping one leg to the ground, inviting me to sit with him. How else will he massage my shoulders? Deep breaths and a prayer that I don't climax from his touch, give me the strength to accept his offer.

Nathan sits at the opposite end of the couch, and I kind of feel bad that he's left out of our contact. Which is utterly ridiculous. It's only a kind gesture.

I let Carson continue his efforts over my entire back and down my arms. The man is a god. The tension in my shoulders is long gone but it's replaced by a knot low in my belly that's wound so hard I'm in pain.

"I need to get a drink. Want popcorn?" he asks.

"Extra butter?"

Nathan agrees, "There's no other way to eat it."

Carson slides out from around me and I fall back onto the arm of the couch when he's gone. I'm kind of drunk on desire after the amazing rub down.

Flopping onto my side, I stretch and intend to rub my foot over Nathan's blanket-covered leg. I overshoot, gliding my foot over the top of his thigh. It's immediately clear that the hard as steel length my toes brush over isn't his leg.

Wet heat soaks my panties. I don't normally use my foot to measure things, but his shaft was...substantial. My sex clenches around emptiness, begging to find out how he would stretch me. The Rolling Stones song about can't get no satisfaction wouldn't exist if all men were built like Nathan.

My eyes dart to his, which have gone wide. Time must have slowed because I take in every flinch in his expression. Every hint of panic. Every shred of embarrassment. His hands move in slow motion, gripping my foot, moving it off his lap.

"Nathan." What am I going to say? I want you to fuck me. One time.

"We can't."

"We can." I do my best not to sound like I'm begging. Who better to take my virginity than a trusted friend?

The feral darkness in his eyes betrays his truth. His actions show his restraint. Time accelerates. He stands. Before I know it, he's on the stairs.

"Finish without me. I'm going to bed."

Ten

Nathan

We're going to have to let her go. It's the only rational thing to do unless I'm going to use my next erection for more than my own entertainment.

I pace back and forth on the deck outside of my bedroom and stare at the bright stars strewn across the blackness. The wee hours of the morning are usually the most peaceful time of day. They hold the answers when my brain won't let go of a problem.

I once thought there was nothing more beautiful than the Milky Way streaking across the sky. It was reserved for those of us who appreciate natural beauty and make it our focus by living in the mountains where man-made lights and wonders are few and far between. Ironic for an architect.

Then Zoe appeared on our roof. I haven't been the same since. Her natural beauty outshines the stars.

I can't figure out any way to keep her in our house and not be obsessed with breeding her. I'd like to think my willpower is stronger than craving such basic needs.

I'd even considered running with the testosterone-driven decision. Not my most glorious moment.

But my heart weighed in and that's when the trouble started. Zoe's a great person, always has been, if not a little weird at points. Fuck, I try to take our history out of the equation. Her avoidance of talking about college had stirred every protective bone in my body.

She needs someone to take care of her, I sense it. I just don't understand why? Which is why I'm certain that one time with her will never be enough. Once I make love to her, I'll commit myself to being everything she ever needs. A provider. A protector. A friend. I want to be Zoe's entire world. I want it more than I want my own success—and that is terrifying.

How can I be everything for someone when I haven't made room in my life for a single day of vacation?

Gripping the top rail of the deck, I lean out, willing some entity in the universe to give me a better answer. The only way I can see to make this right is by paying her the full amount we agreed on and asking Skylar never to send her to my house again.

Instead, every fiber of my being sees the benefit of one time with Zoe—a secret to keep the rest of my life. If I understood how to do it and walk away, I would. Will I break? Or will I hurt the only woman I've considered letting into my life? I don't want to be a one-and-done kind of guy, but with her, I have to. That doesn't even begin to assess how I'd deal with Carson.

He has it as bad for her as I do. His need to protect Zoe already broke through the surface. When he told me what he'd done outside, we agreed that he had to apologize and never lose control again. Then he gave her a shoulder rub. How had he not nutted?

This brings up yet another complication. I liked watching him touch her. I want to feel her moan on my cock while he fucks her to orgasm. I want to spray my cum deep inside of her then have Carson do the same. I want to watch her belly grow. I want to believe that the baby belongs to all of us.

That's the most fucked up thought I've ever had.

A click from overhead catches my attention. I angle my head to the stars, listening as more sounds indicate someone is on the roof deck. If we were anywhere else, I would have missed these subtle sounds. But we're here, in a secluded canyon. Nothing to mar the natural silence—except a faint hum coming from above.

Her intoxicating moans whisp on the breeze. I should go inside. I can't. I'm enthralled then her moans pitch higher and she lets go.

Forcing a retreat into my bedroom, I should get back in bed. I should allow my live-in employee privacy. I should keep my life simple.

But I don't.

I head straight to Carson's room. He's awake. No one's getting any sleep with all of the sexual tension between us. I know what I have to do.

"She's on the roof. Must not have liked getting called out for using a vibrator in the middle of the night." I can't believe what I'm about to propose.

Carson rubs a hand over his face. "I wasn't going to say anything, but it's like I'm in a fucking trance when I'm around her."

"Same thing happens to me. I can't take it anymore."

"So what are you proposing?"

Nothing like a negotiation in a dimly-lit hallway between two horny guys while the woman of their dreams is masturbating on their roof.

"We pay her everything we agreed to but ask her to leave."

"What?"

"I can't do this. I would lose my mind if you hooked up with her. It's the only way."

"What if she agreed to both of us?"

"What do you mean?" I fear letting my thoughts out. I have to hear the words fall from his lips.

"If you say no, I'll drop the whole thing. Pretend this never happened. I respect our relationship too much to let anything come between us, so be honest with me."

"Okay."

"Let's see if she's interested in a threesome. If we all agree to keep it quiet, no one has to know, and maybe we can all finally get some sleep."

"Then what?"

"I can't think clearly enough to figure that out yet."

"What if she's grossed out that we have history? Would you hate me for cock-blocking?"

"When I brought up hearing her through the wall, she looked at you, not me."

"She was probably embarrassed."

"No. I saw the spark in her eyes. She hoped you heard her too. She checks out your ass when she thinks no one's looking. She checks out your cock, too. She respects you and wants you."

"I've noticed her do the same to you."

"She wants both of us."

"This could go seriously wrong."

"It already has."

We stare at each other for a few seconds. He's right. This is already fucked up.

I pound a fist into the wall. "I can't be the one to approach her. And I don't think we should just barge onto the roof while she's..." Fuck, my dick hardens at the thought of Zoe filling her pussy with anything other than Carson or me.

The door to the stairs swings open.

Eleven

Zoe

Sneaking onto the roof for a late-night orgasm had seemed a safe way to put a dent in my cravings without waking the guys up again. The crisp air with the stars overhead offered the perfect solitude for my forbidden pleasures.

Padding downstairs, I ease the lower door open, ready to tiptoe to my bedroom.

I stop dead in my tracks. Carson and Nathan are staring at me from Carson's doorway.

Nathan's sweatpants are slung low on his hips. In the faint light, I make out the outline of his cock. Carson's hair is mussed like he's run his hands through it repeatedly.

Their expressions speak of desire. My rooftop session proves completely inadequate. Does Natalie have to know? Does she get a say?

A second too late, I remember that I'm holding my bright pink vibrator. Both men notice it, their expressions growing more tense. I hide it behind my back anyway.

Is that disappointment that flashes over Carson's face? What can I say? They have to understand that a girl has needs.

He steps forward, reaching behind my back. I want to die. Not really. I want him to grab my ass and pull me tight. Is he as hard and hung as Nathan? Am I depraved? I should be thinking about how to keep my job. Employers rarely like it when you wake them up in the middle of the night every night.

I crane my neck to escape the lure of dragging my fingers through his chest hair. He looks down at me from inches away. There's not enough air for both of us.

His hand slides along my arm. I'm paralyzed for all the wrong reasons. I want my best friend's brothers to fuck me. I want to see the possessiveness in Carson's eyes again. I want them to loom over me while they decide how to take me.

His large hand closes over mine. His fingers wedge between mine, one at a time, shoving mine out of the way. He tucks his thumb around my wrist, keeping my hand in his possession. My only movement is me swallowing mortification.

I'd love to wake up from a dream right about now. I get the message. Stop masturbating in their house. My body grows hotter. I don't think it's a dream.

Carson's free hand slips into mine. I can't see Nathan with Carson standing so close. Will he be able to keep Carson calm? My breaths are audible. I wish he'd just get it over with and fire me.

"You shouldn't be using this." Carson's voice is low and haggard as he brings the pink penis beside us. "Besides, it's not big enough."

Did he just say... No time to think. He guides my hand to his erection.

He's right.

"I'll stop. I promise to control myself."

Well, that sounded stupid. The lack of oxygen must be getting to me.

"We don't want you to control yourself. When you blush at innuendo, when we catch you looking at us, and when we hear you pleasing yourself in the middle of the night, we barely stay in control. What if we all stopped?"

Are my ears deceiving me? I lean to the side so I can see Nathan. He steps closer. Closer than ever before. Willpower drains from me, making it hard to keep from running my fingers over the line of hair from his belly button into his sweats.

Nathan shocks me with his offer. "One night. One secret. One—"

"No," Carson booms, gripping my hand tighter. I hear my vibrator fall to the ground as he reaches behind my head, tangling his fingers in my hair. I think he's shutting down when he repositions his hand between us, cupping my tender sex.

My already troubled breaths hitch. Satisfaction will be in huge supply with these two.

I shiver with need as he continues, "It can't be one night. Not with the way Goldie drives me crazy with every breath she takes."

Can he truly need me that badly? I'd doubt it if I didn't feel the same toward them.

His hand stays firm against me. I want him to know it's okay, so I squeeze his cock. He huffs a laugh and lowers his head. "Good girl," he whispers into my ear.

Fuck. Is it possible to orgasm from words? My bones liquefy.

"One night then we re-evaluate." Is he more worried about how a ménage relationship would reflect on him professionally or at least in town, or just Natalie's reaction? She's so sweet and innocent. She'll never understand, which is exactly why this is best kept a secret.

"I agree." Lovely. What do I think we're doing, taking a vote? Hmm, we kind of are. Consent and communication will be important.

Carson's hand tugs at my hair, angling my mouth upward. His lips part and he pauses. My sanity dangles by a thread.

Carson leans close. "Are you sure?"

"Yes."

Nathan drops his gaze to the floor. "Both of us?"

"Yes."

Leaving his head lowered, he lifts his eyes to meet mine. "Even if doing so would ruin the nice, big brother image you have of me?"

I don't worry that he'll ruin my image of him. I'm worried he'll ruin me. I'm worried I'll hang on to the sound of my name on his lips in the heat of passion, the primal utterance of his release, and the heavy breaths that will only warm my skin for one night.

It will all be worth it.

Our eyes are locked, both testing the line we shouldn't cross.

The slightest shake of his head confuses me. Is he telling me to resist? He's not in charge of me. I've spent too long letting other people control what I do. Tonight, I'm making my own choice. No one has to know. The only thing that will change is me taking control of my own life. Going after what I want.

I nod agreement. "How big are you?"

His eyes go dark and he swallows hard, but neither of us moves.

It's Carson who seizes the moment. His mouth claims me. The kiss is so deep I lose track of myself. It's only when the cool night air hits me that I realize I'm in his arms, we've gone up the stairs and Nathan has opened the door to the roof.

When Carson lets me up for air, Nathan slides his arms around me, turning my body so that my legs straddle his waist. "This is our secret."

I nod understanding. We're on the side of the rooftop deck that isn't visible by neighbors, where I'd moved the chair to. I've kept my attraction to him secret for years, but this is so different. What have I become?

Our mouths mesh as if every fantasy he's starred in has shown us the path to each other. That I already know him and he knows me in the most intimate ways.

"Where were you when you pleased yourself?" Carson asks.

"On the chair." I'm struggling to answer Carson's questions while Nathan kisses my neck and shoulders, and everywhere he can get his mouth on me while rubbing me up and down his length.

"Did you take your shorts off?"

"No, I scooted them to the side."

"Did you spread your legs wide to open that sweet pussy for your fake cock?"

"Yes," I whimper between kisses, suddenly aware that I'm grinding against Nathan's thickness.

He brings his lips to my ear. "Show us how you did it."

Is this normal? Foolish question. The better one is where did my inhibitions go? I want Carson and Nathan to keep telling me what to do. I want to please them. And I want to find out what the look in their eyes translates to in terms of orgasms.

Nathan sets me on the chair, the head raised slightly. I bring my knees up, hooking my feet on the edges of the wood. With my legs spread, the wetness of my panties becomes apparent. I glance at Nathan's crotch, which is easy since he's standing so close beside me. I soaked him. Instead of being embarrassed, the wet spot overlapping his erection encourages me.

He rubs a hand over it, gripping it while I gawk, then moves his hand to my knee.

Carson's eyes lock with mine and he steps to the end of the chair. His features are obscured but his posture doesn't waver.

"Show me how you reached between your legs." Carson's demand is perfect.

I rest my hand on my thigh, giving myself one last out. I don't take it. I've never done this in front of anyone. Never knew I'd want to. Their need fuels me.

My fingers slide down and push the fabric aside. Rather than pretend I'm holding the vibrator, I settle my fingers against my sex.

Gentle pressure has my hips bucking. This has to be one of those dreams I can't wake up from. The kind that goes on all night long. I run with it.

"I want you wider. Drop your feet to the ground the way you did when we first found you up here. The way you've been when I've jerked off to you ever since." Carson doesn't mince words, but is he exaggerating? Has he really...?

Nathan tugs on the knee he's touching, tucking his fingers around it as he helps me lower my leg. I manage the other one on my own.

"That's not going to work. Take your shorts off."

I scramble my legs back onto the chair eager to please when Nathan drops to his knees and adds, "You don't have to do

183

anything you don't want to. No pressure. No repercussions if you decide to stop."

"Thank you," I lift my hips and Nathan takes the cue to remove my shorts. Carson motions for Nathan to toss them to him and he does.

Nathan runs his fingers around the waistband of my panties. "We're going to have to get rid of these too."

My eyes fall shut as I lift my hips again. His fingers ease into the elastic, brushing against my skin, driving me to the brink of orgasm without even touching my curls.

Thank god I shaved. The humorous thought of our first encounter could have been quite different if I'd spread my legs and exposed the rainforest. Would they have still been interested? I stifle a chuckle as Nathan's fingers stay in contact with my skin to the tips of my toes.

He balls the fabric in one hand and teases a finger from the other hand over my inner thigh. "I'm keeping these."

Is there a proper response? It's easier not to talk, and just ease my legs around the chair again. Anything to get this show on the road.

"Do you care who goes first?"

"Either one." How could I possibly pick? Alphabetical order? Age? There's no logical way.

"You go ahead," Nathan says, and drags his finger through my juices then trails them up my belly, sliding his hand into my shirt. He toys with my nipple, sending excitement through me.

"Your breasts are perfect. I've wanted to play with these little nipples ever since they beaded when we caught you up here. I imagined my tongue on them. Did you know what you were doing to me?"

"I thought I was in trouble," I answer honestly. Why am I so turned on that he reacted that way?

"And they kept poking against your shirts the last few days. I can't even jack off enough to get rid of the blue balls you cause." He drops his mouth, pulling my top up, teasing my nipple with his tongue. My back arches off the cushion. Then he kisses, laps, and flicks me into near oblivion.

"I was going to watch for a minute, but I can't let you make her come without me." Carson's voice sends an extra surge through me. I'm dangerously close to losing control.

My eyes are closed but the warmth of Carson's hands caressing up my legs, having both of them touch me at the same time, is too much.

I cry out, all coherency lost, as I clamp my legs against the chair. An orgasm rips through me. I wouldn't believe it could happen without either of them touching my sex.

Hot breath high on my inner thigh draws me back from bliss. Am I ready for this?

A hand is on my belly and it takes me a second to place it as Nathan's.

"You should have warned us you were that needy, Goldie. We could have taken care of you sooner." Nathan surprises me with the use of my nickname, and the blatant call-out.

I don't have time to respond. Carson kisses my sex, locking in the start of my next orgasm.

Nathan claims my mouth. Carson's tongue slides over my clit and I lose focus. No longer able to think about what I should be doing, I simply exist at the hands and mouths of my soon-to-be lovers.

My body's wound with need. I'm giving and taking. One hand is tangled in Carson's hair, holding him close. The other explores Nathan's bare chest, arms, and back. But there's no plan, no intent, just passion.

Carson's tongue makes one final stroke, pushing me to the point of no return. My moan is swallowed by Nathan's kiss. I'm consumed by the climax, thrown so far into euphoria that I barely register the guys swapping positions.

Nathan peppers my belly with kisses. I stare up at the stars, wondering how I ended up with these two out of everyone in the universe, and if there's any way we can make this more than a one-time thing?

Nathan licks my next orgasm into a frenzy. I'm about to fall again when he stops. I'm panting, craving, desperate. I buck my hips.

"I'm almost there."

"I'll get you there after I'm sure it will be the biggest one you've ever had." He leans back in, alternating kissing and licking, pausing and repeating. I'm about to lose my mind.

Then it hits me that I haven't done anything for them. Oh no. I can't mess this up. Carson's lip-lock has him distracted, so I run my hand down his side, finding his erection. I stroke his length three times before he pulls my hand away.

His lips barely lift. "Not yet."

I can't imagine what's wrong with now, but his mouth is back on mine.

Does Nathan sense that I can't take anymore? He's all in on eating my pussy when I lose control. My hips thrust into him. I fist his hair, trying to get him closer. Yet, as huge and blinding as my climax is, I crave being filled by a cock.

Carson cups a hand behind my head and deepens our kiss then nothing matters. Every need I've ever ignored, every attraction that's been unrequited, and every fantasy I've ever thought I fulfilled splinter apart. I'm everything. I'm sated. I'm theirs.

Both of my legs are being moved onto the chair when I drift back. There's a sense that they're handling something precious. Me. For all of the craziness and lust, they must feel the deeper connection too.

"Sweet Goldie, what are we going to do with you?"

I roll my head toward Carson who's on the opposite side from Nathan.

He moves errant strands of hair behind my ear. I lick my lips trying to get my bearings. What to do with me? How about finishing what we started? I'm too sex drunk to speak.

Hands slide under me and I turn to Nathan, who says, "We better get you a bath and put you to bed."

"But we didn't finish. You guys—"

"Not tonight. We want to make sure you're okay with this before we go any further."

I'm limp in his arms as he lifts me. "I want this. I want you...both."

"And if you still want to, we can."

Carson makes the decision definitive. "For now we need to take care of you and let you rest. I'm going to get a bath ready."

He plants the sweetest kiss on my cheek then leads the way inside.

"And don't worry about breakfast, I'm placing an order from the diner," he calls over his shoulder.

I'm so spent I can't argue. I'm not turning down a bath. Snuggling into Nathan's chest I only have one care in the world. I won't change my mind, but what if they do?

Nathan hugs me tighter as we descend the stairwell.

Please don't let anyone come to their senses. Another flicker of worry crosses my mind. What if I'm feeding the dependency I'm working so hard to overcome?

It doesn't matter because nothing's ever felt so right.

Twelve

Zoe

Sleeping in my own bed gave me plenty of time to consider what happened and what *could* happen.

My initial reaction to Nathan's insistence we slow down had been confusion, then fear that he changed his mind about going further. But they were so sweet and tender bathing me and making sure I was tucked in. My myriad thoughts transitioned to happiness and comfort.

It's happening fast and I think that scares all of us. Giving our thoughts and emotions a day to settle is the right thing to do.

I hadn't been able to sleep in, and they'd insisted on having breakfast delivered, so I'm curled up on the couch when Nathan comes down.

"Hey." His sheepish grin matches my nerves.

"Hey." Will everything be fine between us?

He strides to the kitchen for water. With the bar between us, he says, "You okay? I mean, after last night. Do you have any concerns?"

How sweet. "I'm more than okay."

Carson's laugh comes from the stairwell. "Then we're on for tonight?"

He walks straight to me and kisses the top of my head.

My hand brushes over his scruff as he pulls away. Looking up at him, we're lost in happiness as I say, "I can't believe you're going to make me wait."

Nathan joins us. "It's best not to rush things."

Carson winks at me. "Yeah, we don't want to rush things."

Rush must be a relative term.

This feels more like home than anything. Even more than the actual home I'd grown up in. The atmosphere was always ripe with expectations and goals. I never had any power.

Breakfast arrives and I lament that the guys eat quickly before a virtual meeting with their client. The day is set into motion, and I'm surprised that I really have to wait. I don't want to come across as a petulant child. With them being older than me, it's crossed my mind that our age gap could be an issue.

While I'm taking the packaging from breakfast out to the trash can, I see Madison waving from a couple houses down.

"Hi, Zoe. I heard you were living, I mean working in Eggplant Canyon. Want to come over and hang out?"

So, word's gotten around that I'm working here. The rumor mill is astounding sometimes, but since Madison was one of the popular kids who kept up with everyone's business, it shouldn't surprise me that she's heard.

Glancing back at the massive log cabin, and considering the small amount of work I have scheduled for today, I take the offer for some girl time. No need to let high school hierarchy get in the way.

We settle on a time that allows me to get ready. Since the guys are holed up in their office, it shouldn't be a problem.

I'm about to head out when Carson's voice booms from his office. "Are you going somewhere?"

His possessive tone is back.

I love that he's protective of me but worry that the comfort comes from the wrong place—years of conditioning. "I'm meeting a friend who moved back home across the lake."

The term friend might be a stretch but we're more than acquaintances.

The light coming through his office door is cut off as his large frame takes up most of the doorway. "Which friend?"

"Madison Shepherd. She's a teacher. Moved back home to take the position that's open."

His shoulders relax as soon as I say her name. Was he jealous that it might be a guy? Interesting.

"I'll get all of my work done. I promise."

He motions with his pointer finger for me to come to him. In a heartbeat, he hoists me up. "Behave."

Then he kisses my lips like we're in the heat of passion. I reflexively grind against his jeans, but he stills my hips. "Like I said. Behave. None of that until tonight."

Nathan joins us in the doorway for a kiss then with a swat of my bottom, I'm returned to my feet and set out to see a friend.

I show up right on time and she bounces as she hands me a cappuccino. Has she had a few too many already?

"I'm so glad you came over."

"Thanks for the invite. I've only been back in town a few days and haven't had a chance to reconnect with anyone."

Madison bites her lower lip. "You moved in with Carson and Nathan. Seems that you're finding plenty of fun." She raises her eyebrows.

I hold my cup in front of my mouth. How do I reply to that? Do they have a reputation? "I'm working for Skylar's maid service and they hired me to be a live-in for two weeks. Some big project is taking up all of their time."

I downplay the extent of our relationship.

"But they're super hot. And rich. Or didn't you notice? You never dated in high school, did you?"

We're in uncomfortable territory but owning my past is part of establishing the new me. "I wasn't allowed to date."

"Oh. That's weird. So do you date now?"

"Yeah." And I'd rather not talk about my dating life. "But hey, you're back in town, anything exciting going on?"

She beams, and shuffles in her oversized deck chair to get her feet under herself. "Very...it's still sort of a secret."

"Secret?" I've never been the type of person people tell secrets to. I'd keep them safe but my upbringing didn't exactly lend itself to having close friends.

She waves her hand toward my house. "Well, since you're...a maid...for them, I figure we can swap secrets."

How can she possibly know? I settle my back against the cushion, attempting to appear unfazed. She's probably just fishing.

As I assumed would happen, she continues, "I'm in a relationship with my ex's dad and his friend."

I'm suddenly not ready to have this conversation. Distraction needed. "I'm going shopping this afternoon. I need to pick up some stuff for the online bartending class I'm taking. Want to go with me?"

"Only if you'll admit that you're more than their maid..."

Wow, she pulls out all the stops. The guys and I agreed not to tell anyone. "Nothing official." I wink to let her feel like she has information without divulging any more.

My offer is enough to patch us over, but guilt racks me that my not-really-anything admission will come back to haunt me.

Thirteen

Carson

Not only did Goldie visit with a neighbor's daughter this morning, but she's also out shopping with her now. Why does that bother me? Why do I want to be the center of her world?

The cold hard reality is that she's several years younger than me and wants more out of life than sitting at a desk. Am I foolish to think that what we have is anything more than a few weeks of fun?

If Nathan hadn't ended things last night, I would have gone all the way. That's not how I should act if I want a relationship. I hid my irritation, but I'm glad he cut us off. We all need to think about this.

More would mean longer term, going public, telling our sister... Can we handle that? Can Goldie?

Will she be able to tolerate us for more than two weeks? My chest tightens as I open the project scheduler on my computer screen. So few days, and nights.

"It's tight, but we can do it." Did Nathan read my mind? He continues, "The timeline."

Swiveling around to face him, I open up. "I'm not worried about the job. We'll get it done. We always do."

"That's how we got our 'balls to the walls' reputation."

"Yeah, our clients love us. We love our jobs. It's been great, but do you ever want more?"

"Is this about Zoe?"

Nathan's phone buzzes. He grabs it, shakes his head, and taps on the screen. "Just a second."

He exchanges a few messages with whoever it is, leaving me to decide how to address the Zoe issue.

Am I crazy to think she's my future when I haven't even made love to her? A threesome...not exactly the kind of relationship that screams that this is forever. I tap my fingers on the arms of my chair.

Setting his phone on his desk, he turns his attention back to me. "That was Natalie. I swear she has sibling radar."

"What did she say?"

He's too calm for Natalie to know anything.

"Had me worried for a minute. Just mentioned she wanted to swing by sometime and make sure we're not being too hard on Zoe."

I raise my eyebrows. Panic races through me that she could turn this into a deal breaker.

Nathan elaborates, "Don't worry, she just didn't want us leaving dirty underwear laying around."

"Right. No way Zoe would have said anything. But hey, I've kind of been wondering...do you think this will just be a one-time thing? We said that and then already blew it by adding the re-evaluate step."

He crosses his arms then balls a fist and bumps it on his lips. His focus is somewhere on the floor. I give him time to process, and after a few long seconds, he lifts his eyes to meet mine and says, "It has to be."

"What if I want more?" My palms sweat. I drag them over my thighs.

"How much more?"

"More."

Nathan shakes his head. "We don't have time for a relationship. This has to stay casual."

"Do you really think it will?"

He stares at the doorway. I think he's mainly avoiding looking at me. I'll see right through his lie.

Nathan's tone is heavy. "I almost lost control last night, that's why I had to cut it off. I don't think Zoe's ready for how hard I want to fuck her. I want to mark her with my damn cum. I can't settle for a fling. It's too risky."

"What's the risk? We piss off our sister? Goldie pisses off her friend?"

"Keeping a secret from Natalie is one thing. Not a problem. Admitting that we had a three-way with her best friend...that's the part I can't do. Not with the way I want to bathe myself in Zoe's juices. Natalie always hated the way her friends acted around me. I've tried to repair our relationship. This would be a major setback. If you lived with us, you'd understand."

"Would I? You think I can hold back any easier than you when all I can think about are the things Zoe does to my heart? Feelings, man. Real fucking feelings." And there it is, I dumped it on Nathan.

He rocks back in his chair, his jaw falling slack. "Feelings in your heart?"

I shrug it off. "Yeah, I'm not afraid to admit it. I want more than one time or a fling with Goldie."

"Fuck, I knew this was a bad idea."

"Opt out." The truth is I like his involvement. I've never thought of Nathan in a sexual sense, but I loved tag-teaming Goldie with him. It is a huge part of the excitement. Correction, Goldie was by far the main attraction, but Nathan added something positive I hadn't expected.

The stone-cold expression on his face consumes several seconds. He doesn't have to say anything for me to know that last night rocked his world. He ate her pussy like his life depended on it. And he edged her, drawing it out until I was about to nut just from watching.

I wasn't complaining about the extra time to play with her tits and kiss her while her juices were still on my mouth. But a guy's not going to draw out a woman's orgasm unless he's enjoying it.

I press him. "Shoot straight. If our sister wasn't in the picture, would you question this?"

"Yeah, I would. Our professional reputation could be at stake. How would we handle interviews or town gossip or treating her the way she deserves to be treated?"

"Fuck what everyone says. We have more requests from clients than we can handle. So what if a few jackasses judge us?"

Nathan turns to his computer and searches for something. "Four to five percent of Americans practice polygamy. Do you think those people are our future clients who won't judge us?"

I scoot close enough to read the screen. "But twenty percent have practiced it at some time in their lives."

"Want to take bets on how many of those are drunken college situations? Zoe may not have been drunk last night but she is in college. We're not. That statistic isn't for functional, long-term relationships."

I punch his arm playfully. "So you admit that you want a relationship."

He crosses his arms. "I didn't admit anything."

"Then why make the distinction? Why can't we play this out, and let Goldie choose? If it's just experimental college fun for her, we know it will end."

"And what about those *feelings* you mentioned?" Nathan taunts me.

"Fuck off."

"You're not going to mope around like a sad puppy, are you?" Nathan cracks himself up.

"I can handle it." That's the only lie I've ever told Nathan. My stomach knots, but I think it's more out of concern that he might be right. This could be a college-aged experiment for Goldie. I'm not sure I can deal with that.

Fourteen

Nathan

Zoe's been home for a couple of hours by the time we finish work. This client is turning into a real pain in the ass, which we should have figured when they insisted we shave two weeks off the timeline.

Now if only they'd answer all of the questions we sent them. We can't move forward with some of the designs until they do.

But even workaholics need a break, and Zoe has dinner ready. Too bad it's only for us adults and not a brood of kids too. I'm way ahead of myself.

The big question will be if she's still game for sex. A storm rages outside, giving the evening an isolated, cozy feel as darkness surrounds the house and rain pelts the windows.

There's a rumble so hard it shakes the entire house. Seemed like more than thunder but it's probably just a result of my nerves being on edge.

We head downstairs, the scent of fresh bread making me even hungrier than I am. Neither of us mentions the looming question. Despite the promise this evening holds, the thought of sitting across the table from Zoe, talking with her and Carson, and finding out how her day went, has me the most excited.

I can't go so far as to say I'm not amped about finishing what we started, but if she wanted to snuggle on the couch first and watch a movie, I'd do it. No more sitting at the opposite end denying my attraction to her.

Carson and I have been a unit for a long time. I never considered that someone might fit with us so naturally.

A different cocktail awaits us at each place setting.

I stop a few paces away from the table. Now that we put time between the impromptu lust of the night before, does she need to get drunk to have another go? Hope sinks away from me. I replay my words from earlier.

How many of those are drunken college situations?

I can't be a regret.

"Drinks...that's a surprise."

"Tell me what you think. We can share. And give me your honest feedback on how I did."

Share? Honest feedback on how she did?

Carson picks up what appears to be a martini garnished with lemon.

"Wait."

His hand halts midway to his mouth.

"Why did you make drinks?" Barring the obvious...adults tend to enjoy them.

"I'm practicing my mixology skills." She lifts a jigger. "I bought a few things this afternoon so I could outfit your kitchen to mix drinks, and I want you guys to be honest. I know there's more to bartending than mixing drinks, but I have to start somewhere."

"You're studying to be a bartender?" Carson asks bluntly.

Her smile fades. "The hours won't interfere with other jobs or classes and I should be able to make good money. My friend, Mammoth is a bartender. He said he could hire me."

"Guys will be hitting on you." He doesn't let up. Fuck. Why am I pretending there's any way this can work?

"I suppose."

"I don't like that." He sets the glass down.

She stares at him curiously as he stalks toward her.

He pins her against the counter, his hands on either side.

"You can't know you don't like it, you didn't even try it," she teases.

I love watching Carson be so dominant. Is it weird that I'm turned on by their interaction?

The growl in his tone is even better. "I don't like guys hitting on you."

"It wouldn't mean anything."

"It would to them. I know what would be going on in their minds."

"Oh really?"

Damn. This is our chance to let this evening happen naturally. No alcohol-reduced inhibitions. She's either in this or not. I rush beside them.

I tuck a finger under her chin, angling her face to mine. "Most guys wouldn't be willing to stop and give you time to make sure you're not making a decision that you'll regret later."

"I didn't ask for time, you did."

"He did because he's a gentleman." Carson defends me.

My phone buzzes...my sister, Natalie. Perhaps it's guilt that makes me take the call, but I tell her now's not a good time, and return my attention to the immediate situation. Nothing can mar this evening. I step back to Zoe and Carson.

She has one hand on my chest and the other on his. "I haven't changed my mind. And since you broke my vibrator when you dropped it, you're going to have to take care of me."

He lifts her onto the counter and positions himself between her legs. Her skirt rode up but he's close enough that it bunches even more. "I have every intention of taking care of you."

"Right here?"

"Have you ever done it on a counter?"

"No." She doesn't have to think about it.

How many times has she had sex? I know I should ask. I don't.

"You don't have to do this." Do I sound like a broken record? I don't want to make things weird, but fucking her is. Why does my dream girl have to be Zoe? Will she tell Natalie we're sexual deviants if she realizes I want to knock her up with at least triplets?

She seems to be thinking about what she would say no to then blurts, "I want to."

In theory, it's easier for me to let Carson go first since he's between her legs. He's already dropping his pants and scooting her to the edge.

My cock nearly busts through my jeans. "You're not wearing any panties."

Stating the obvious is rarely useful, but I can't stop myself.

Carson laughs as he brushes a thumb over her curls.

She bites her lower lip and wrinkles her brow. "I wanted to know what it felt like."

There's no stopping myself. Gently tugging, I guide her legs wider. My fingers dip toward the already wet curls surrounding the milky white juices coating her tight opening. I extend a finger, wetting it in her excitement. Oh fuck, I'm in trouble.

Carson positions his cock at her entrance. "Is it okay if he plays with your sweet spot while I stroke you from the inside?"

"I think so. I've never done this before." The softness in her tone makes me suspect a threesome isn't the only thing she hasn't done.

I kiss her lips while circling a finger over her clit. She's hungry. I decide to run with it. "Neither have we. Are you ready?"

She nods but her kiss tightens.

I lean away and look down. Carson's tip has pushed past her pussy lips. "Hold on."

They both look at me like I've lost my mind. I force my hand to her thigh.

I can't let this go. "Are you a virgin?"

Why is there a pause? Every muscle in my body tenses. Her first time can't be like this. How the hell can I get Carson to take his dick out of her?

"I'm not." Her answer is so timid I don't trust her.

Carson has to understand what I'm getting at. Based on his tip inching forward, I'm guessing he's taking her word for it.

Fuck. Fuck. Fuck.

He'll hate me if I ruin this. Shit. I'll hate myself.

"I don't mean just with a vibrator. Have you had a cock inside of you?" Doesn't that sound patronizing? If we could go back to the rooftop the first day, I'd tell the maid service we need a replacement for the replacement.

"Yes." The single word. The three letters of it. The breath that she says it on...they're angel's voices, wishes being granted, and friendships saved.

Carson looks me dead in the eye. "You done with the interrogation?"

In my periphery, his hips push forward. His expression shifts to pure bliss. I can't believe what we're doing. That I'm watching two people have sex. Way more intimate than porn.

Way more dangerous because I have attachments to both of them. Way out of my comfort zone.

But when I look into Zoe's eyes, a woman full of needs looks back at me. This is Goldie. Am I an ass for having to use this nickname, this persona? She's still Zoe, our sister's best friend.

And I want her more than I can handle.

She's not saying no.

Thunder cracks, the lights flicker off, and the electronic displays on the appliances go dark. The power must have gone out. A second later, everything kicks back on thanks to the backup generator we installed.

I should check that everything's okay, but Zoe's more important.

I slide my hand back to her clit, and Carson shifts his hand from her hip to her thigh so I can move closer. My fingers brush against his cock as he makes slow, short strokes. I reposition. Alternating kissing Zoe and watching our triple union, my cock and balls are begging for breathing room.

Without missing a beat, I unzip my pants and shuck them off. My underwear's a little more difficult, but I get it.

The strange acceptance of what we're doing hits me again. Why am I not bothered by the incidental touches of his cock? Goldie's breaths heighten as her clit hardens and swells under my fingers.

He's got to be in pain. And Goldie's going to make him feel better. Then I'll give her another orgasm. This three-way dynamic is special. I've never had thoughts like this. I've never banged one of my sister's friends. I've never been so turned on by watching.

Zoe clamps a hand over mine and her cries ring through my mind. She's about to climax. I can't take my eyes off of her mouth hanging open and her eyes lidded with lust as I keep the rhythm she guides me to.

Her fingers tighten, and Carson pumps hard, driving our joined hands harder and harder against her clit. Then her eyes fall shut, her body lurches, and she comes apart in my hand. It's the most beautiful thing I've ever seen.

Carson's hand that has been on her thigh, grips my arm. Does he realize what he's doing? The strength of his grasp would bruise her. I'm glad to be taking the brunt of it. I'm more than glad.

Her release, the throb of his cock, and the scent of sex shove me over the edge. There's nothing for me to hold onto as I blow my load over both of them.

Her thigh, her belly, and on Carson. I've fucking marked them.

Shouldn't I want to run? Hide? That's not what happens in my brain. They're mine. There's no turning back. When Goldie drags her finger through my release, my cock twitches again, rallying for one more stream onto them.

Her smile is weak but sated, perhaps thinking I'll need recharge time, but it's my turn and I'm not missing it. My cock thickens.

"I'm not done."

She furrows her brow.

"Hop down. I need to feel you."

She nods and Carson helps her down while I sheathe myself.

I spin her around, bending her over the counter. Sinking into her tightness, my cock is harder than when I started. Did she lie about being a virgin? I won't call her out because it doesn't matter now.

Carson leans with her, kissing her while I fuck her and work her clit. I'm not the only one on a hair trigger. Her walls pulse around me. I come so hard my balls threaten to choke me.

This can't be a one-time thing.

I pull her up against my chest and Carson sandwiches her between us. For a few minutes, all we do is exist.

No one moves. Our breaths synchronize. Our bodies mesh. Our bond is secure.

Carrying her onto the side of the private deck that faces the mountain, we each rinse off in the outdoor shower then get in the hot tub.

There's room for eight but she's snuggled between us on one side, the mountain rising in front of us.

Carson is trailing his fingers down the length of her arm to her fingertip, then back up, and repeating it with the next finger. I'm tracing the strands of her hair, watching her profile as she rests her head against Carson's arm. Her eyes are closed. Happiness? I don't want to make a wrong assumption.

"Was that okay?"

She lifts her head with a sleepy smile and curls her arm to rub my chin. "It was even better than I expected."

"What did you expect?" No surprise that Carson would take that statement as some sort of challenge.

Her body wiggles against me as she giggles. "I don't know. I guess I didn't expect to do it on the kitchen counter."

That makes two of us.

"Can I ask you something?" She's timid again.

"Anything," Carson is quick to respond.

I've never seen him like this, in any relationship, with his intensity and eagerness to please. He wasn't kidding about his feelings. Feelings and casual sex don't mix. I'm proof of that.

Every bit of the possessive intensity I see in his expression and the way he treats Zoe is paralleled in me. I don't want this to end.

"In the interest of re-evaluating, would it be okay if we did it again?"

"We're going to do this again." Carson looks at me. We're not going to stop.

The moment is perfect as the wind rustles through the treetops. Our relationship is a minuscule existence against the majesty of the mountain. But the social repercussions are much bigger.

Before Carson gets too far down a rabbit hole of feelings, I say, "How did you decide to switch from college to bartending?"

"I'm not going to let you be a bartender." Carson's comment makes her shrink.

"Hear her out, Carson. You don't have any say in what she does."

He grumbles but kisses the side of her head.

"My parents were only willing to help me pay for college if I studied what they wanted. I didn't get much say in my life growing up."

"Sorry, beautiful." Carson realizes his mistake.

"Now, I have to save up money. Plus, bartending seemed like a fast way to meet people. I don't have many friends and the people I clean for try to ignore me or boss me around."

"I'll talk to them." Carson's on edge.

"No need. It's part of the job."

I'm confused. "You grew up here. Surely you have friends from school."

"Not with parents like mine."

Carson growls and shifts so he can drape his arm over her lap.

"They weren't mean or abusive, they just didn't let me do fun stuff. They controlled everything."

"Then I say we do fun stuff. Lady's choice," Carson says into her lips.

I'm about to clarify that we can't do stuff in town until we agree to take our relationship public, but Goldie climbs onto his lap and we segue into another round of love-making, only all Zoe's agreed to is sex.

The only way to avoid fighting this losing battle is to deny what I feel for Zoe. I don't think I'm physically capable of doing that.

Fifteen

Zoe

I'd thought Carson and Nathan had literally rocked my world, but it turns out the big rumble we felt the first evening we had sex was actually a mudslide. It covered the road, trapping us in Eggplant Canyon.

If only they hadn't had to work so hard to meet their client's request. I made good on deep dive cleaning for them, which is hardly a thing since they're pretty tidy.

One lane of the road is open, but everything I want is right here in their house. Maybe I should go into town to clear my head. Other than a few orgasm-laced proclamations, we all agreed this is sex.

Setting the timer for nine minutes, I hope the chocolate chip cookie smell will put the guys in a better mood.

Nathan just got off another call with their client. He and Carson are grouching about what a prick this guy is. That's the part they agree on. The other part is more complicated. Carson's getting tense because he can't engineer the primary bedroom design until Nathan designs it.

The homeowners want a water feature in the bedroom but Nathan's gone from a fountain, to a waterfall in the corner, to an entire rain wall and they're still not satisfied. With only five days left to finish the plans, Carson's worried he'll end up being the bad guy who'll get blamed for not completing the project on time.

I don't like hearing the guys tense with each other. It reminds me of my parents arguing. At least I'm not the subject.

But I've been the source of tension. The bartending thing had caused tension, and Carson's jealousy over me talking to the neighbor.

Which brings up a great point. Even when they're grumpy or controlling, they're not like my parents. We work things out.

Don't we?

Carson still hasn't agreed to me bartending. He still doesn't want me talking to the neighbors. It seems he wants our relationship to be my whole world, but that's only good for the short time we have left. And now that I see how things have worked out, I wonder if the whole thing about hiring me was a ruse to get me in bed from the start.

Whatever, I'm not complaining.

The question is if our one-time fling morphed into something more, the way I want to believe, or did they design and engineer our relationship?

There are so many problems with *us*.

I hop onto the counter and watch the countdown clock on the oven.

Instead of making adult-level decisions, am I just falling prey to my own conditioning? Letting people control me? It would be easier to accept if I didn't feel so attached to them.

My mind goes back to what we did at this very spot a few days before. I love what I have with them. Their kind of control feeds me. I feel stronger, more secure when they bolster me.

Natalie texts: *We should have a girls weekend.*

Why is my gut reaction to be sad that I'd lose precious time with Carson and Nathan? On the surface, what we have can never work. In my heart, what we have is perfect.

I reply: *Have to plan it around work*

Natalie: *Seriously? I thought you were just filling in.*

I better warn them. Padding to the office, I head to Carson first. He kisses my boob before I get a chance to lean down, then hoists me across his lap. I'm not supposed to bother them but as I duck into their office, I accept the fantasy of our little world.

"Natalie's coming this weekend." I scrunch my shoulders as Carson tickles my neck with kisses.

"Guess we better get busy before she gets here."

"We don't have time for that." Nathan slams his fist on his desk.

I cringe. Not really scared, just surprised. Nathan's usually the level-headed one.

"Just taking a break for a few minutes." Carson hoists me back to standing and swats my ass. "But tonight...you better be ready. Or we could just tell Natalie you're our girlfriend."

"No." Nathan stares at Carson like he's lost his mind. "No girlfriends. No relationships. No commitments. That's how this works. And we're not talking about it during work hours. So if you two don't mind, let's all get back to our jobs. I've got a spoiled millionaire who wants to bring the beach into his bedroom."

The scent of the cookies floats into the room, failing to produce the happy sensation I'd hoped for. No reprieve from Nathan's rant. My role is clear.

"What if you made the waterfall flow under a glass floor? Maybe you could even capture the energy of the falling water to zero out the energy expenditure?" I toss out an idea I've had in my head.

"I don't need help. I need quiet." That's the first time Nathan raised his voice. Do I have two growly bears? Even Carson looks surprised.

Nathan catches himself. "Sorry, I didn't mean to yell at you." He stands, takes my hands, and kisses them, then says, "Are you making cookies?"

"Yep."

"They smell delicious. I'll take a break in a few minutes."

The timer goes off, giving me an easy escape. With the cookies cooling, I go for a walk around the lake. The luxury cabins, the isolation the mountains offer...they're wonderful, but they're temporary, for me. I'm living someone else's dream, and it's good for me to remember that.

As much as it's great for Carson and Nathan to want me to themselves, our arrangement will be over in a few days. I'm taking the job at the bar. I'll stop by and let Mammoth, the bartender know. It wouldn't hurt for me to hang out there for a little bit and make some friends. Real friends who want me for more than their sex toy.

Not that I'm complaining. My worry is how any guy will measure up to what my growly bears have given me. Walking along the edge of the lake, I watch as chipmunks scurry out of my path. I'll miss this place, and how they call me Goldie. I chuckle in disbelief that I've hooked up with two guys. Imagine if the Goldilocks theme had held, what would it have been like to have three growly bears?

"Zoe," A deep, could-be-growly bear voice calls from one of the houses. I tamp down hope that I could find out what getting taken by three men would be like when I turn the direction of the sound and land my gaze on a shirtless version of Jayce, the guy Madison told me about. He's on his deck, his hand raised as he draws my attention in case the mouth-watering chest and abs weren't enough to draw me in.

How does he know my name?

"Hi." I wave and keep walking. Definitely growly bear material, but I won't be sampling him. Madison's claimed that fairy tale.

"Do you have a minute?" His question stops me. Nothing more than politeness so I can respond, but in an alternate reality where naughty happily ever afters existed in a secluded mountain neighborhood, I'd have a lot of minutes available for him.

I cross the street and crane my neck. "Sure, what's up?"

He looks to the side. "It's about..." he lowers his voice. "Madison. I need a woman's advice."

"I'll be right up."

When I get to the top of the deck stairs, he rubs the back of his neck and clears his throat. "Hey, this may come across as kind of weird, but I want to do something nice for Madison."

I'm expecting him to say more, and I'm also stunned by his admission, leaving an awkward silence.

"It's my understanding she told you about our relationship...the three of us?"

I nod too enthusiastically. "Yes,"

"Okay." He scrubs his hands over his face. "We don't exactly have a typical relationship."

A laugh escapes me and I mumble agreement. No judgment from me.

"I want to do something nice for her. Do you have any ideas?"

"Madison loves helping kids. She's volunteering for some of the after-school activities. Maybe do one with her."

Shit! What have I said? He's staring at me like I've just proposed that he turn his entire company over to her.

"Sorry. That's only if you are ready to go public with your relationship." I certainly understand the need for secrets.

"I don't know if she's ready for that, but you're right, she loves helping people. See, this is why I needed your advice. I was going to pull that Hollywood bullshit and have clothes picked out for a date and delivered to her in a big box."

I crack up. "She'd like that too. You just might have to keep the date private until you're ready for everyone to know."

"Yeah, I like that."

Her dad's still going to kill her. That gives me an idea. "I don't mean to overstep, but you and her dad don't get along. That puts her in a tough spot."

"That fucker. Always bitching about one thing or another."

I hold my hands up. "If you truly care about her, you need to patch things up with her dad. Don't make her choose." Ugh, I thought not having to choose between Carson and Nathan was a dream, and it is, but not one I get to keep.

"You're a fucking genius." He wraps me in a giant hug, my face smashed into his chest.

"Oh no, you don't, asshole." Carson's voice calls out unexpectedly.

Jayce's arms fly away from me as Carson and Nathan race toward us. Jayce steps in front of me as they race up the stairs. Probably a bad move, but I appreciate his gesture.

"It's okay." I pat Jayce's arm and step from behind him.

"Don't you try to make a move on her," Carson growls as they storm closer. The possessiveness of his tone takes on an annoying edge.

"I wasn't making a move." Jayce looks from them to me, confusion etched in his features. He's picked up on the tension and looks ready to defend me.

I scramble in front of him before the guys get closer, and throw my hands up. "Nothing is going on. He was asking me for advice, and since I'm nothing more than your maid, you need to stay out of my business."

"Like hell, you're only our maid." Carson's in the growly-bear possessive mode that makes my sex tingle.

My eyes widen at his statement. I lift a finger to my lips to shush him.

"You are our business, our lover, and so much more." Nathan blurts out, adding the reveal to the chaos.

Shit. What do I do now? Jayce stares at me expectantly. I shoot a look at Nathan. It wasn't his place to say anything. I need to be more than someone's little sex toy.

"Are you three..." Jayce's words drop off. A smile takes over his face as he realizes he doesn't have the only scandalous relationship on the block.

"You're in no place to judge. I heard you stole your son's girlfriend," Carson says.

Jayce lunges at Carson and stops himself just short of them throttling each other. "That's not how it happened. Mind your own fucking business."

"I'm their live-in maid. They hired me for two weeks." Will he buy the cover story?

"We want to hire you for a lot more," Carson pleads.

Great, I can be their secret until they're tired of paying for it. This goes way past the issue with Natalie or their clients or even the neighbors. I don't want to be a secret. I deserve more. As painful as it is, I have to do right by me.

"It will never work. I quit. Don't follow me." It's a split-second decision that feels like it took an eternity to play out in my brain. I have to get away from them. I run back to the house.

When I look over my shoulder, Jayce blocks them, giving me a head start. I worry they'll stop me before I back out of the garage. I loved parking in it like I belong, but I don't. And when I realize the guys aren't chasing me, my heart cracks.

It's not that I want to be chased. I want them to care.

Sixteen

Carson

I lose my mind when Goldie leaves. Jayce grabs Nathan and me by the arms, forcing us to stop. I'm tempted to throw a punch and free myself but his words hit home.

"Nothing good will come from chasing her right now. Trust me. She explicitly asked you not to. Respect her space."

"Fuck! Where the hell is she going?" I punch the air. It's not satisfying. If we don't get her back, I'll never be satisfied.

"I don't know what's going on with the three of you, but get your shit together. I've had my share of disasters, learn from my mistakes."

"You don't know what you're talking about." I shrug him off.

"Want to tell me?" Jayce's comment is enough to give me pause. I want to tell him. I want to tell everyone. I can't bear the thought of Goldie choosing anyone or anything but Nathan and me. We're a package deal, and we need her to be complete.

Nathan yanks out of his other hand. I have to respect that the guy could detain both of us. I'm not small, and neither is Nathan. Maybe we knew he was right.

Once we regroup, I'm going to find her and never let her go.

We hash things out with Jayce, share some of his pain in wanting the forbidden fruit, risking judgment. Risking rejection.

Jayce says, "Sneaking around can be fun. But if you love her, it's not right to hide her."

Nathan shakes his head as he paces on the deck. "Why am I so afraid to trust what I'm feeling?"

"Do you love her?" he asks Nathan.

The answer is easy for me. I can't tear my gaze from Nathan as he struggles with the decision. I know that he loves the bubble of fantasy around *Goldie*, but can he deal with the attachments that come with *Zoe*?

"I've got to go home." He heads back to the house without answering.

I give him a few minutes lead, taking time to ask Jayce about his fiasco with Madison, his son's ex-girlfriend. I thought we had a mess, but his scenario is even more twisted.

I can't focus. Where did Zoe go?

We part ways, and when I get back to the house, Nathan's pacing behind the pool table Jayce had recently given us, assessing shot options. He stands the cue in front of himself, grabbing it with both hands at chest level.

"I called and she didn't answer," he confesses. "What if I blew it?"

"We'll talk to her. First, you need to get straight with me though. You didn't answer Jayce's question."

He haphazardly lines the balls up and takes a shot. The crack of the balls slamming together isn't nearly as satisfying when I'm not the one doing it. We both watch a striped ball bounce off the edges before rolling toward the side pocket, teetering, then falling in.

I know better than to press him until the play is complete.

"Do you love her?" We're going to have serious issues if he can't admit it.

"We agreed. No fucking the maid. Then it was one time. Then two. Then two weeks." He lifts a ball out of the pocket and rolls it to the center of the table.

"Your point?" I empty the pockets closest to me.

He sets the rack on the table and starts filling it. "We need order. We need stability. We don't have time for this..." He waves his hand loosely in what I'm assuming he means to indicate a relationship.

"We have time for whatever we choose to have time for."

"Then why haven't we taken a vacation?" He swaps a few stripes and solids, getting them in their proper order, making sure all of the numbers face up.

"We loved our jobs. No need to change that until something better came along."

"Some*thing*? So Zoe's just an object to you? I'll give you benefit of the doubt since you haven't known her long, but she's smart and—"

I slam my hand down on the rack when he tries to lift it. "Don't accuse me of objectifying her. What we have is erotic and primal, but that doesn't make it wrong. At least I'm not afraid to say that I love her."

"Do you?"

"Yes."

"What do you know about her? Can you tell me what she went to school for?"

"Don't pull that bullshit. Things are happening fast. Besides, I don't love her because of whatever degree she pursued or might pursue. I simply love her."

"How can you be sure?" He's asking for himself, not me. His concerns are slipping through the cracks in his façade.

"You know how we used to live for our jobs?"

"Yeah."

"I always knew something was missing. I thought that if I worked hard enough, I'd find it. Even when we got fame and fortune, and everything we wanted, emptiness still plagued me."

"Why didn't you say anything?"

"It made me feel greedy that after all the success we had, I wasn't happy."

"And you're happy now?"

I scoff. "Happy? I found my fucking reason to live."

"What if we land this interview with Engineering Digest? They like to do personal pieces—dive into the lives of the greatest minds in design and engineering."

"Why don't you jump to what you're really worried about?"

Nathan raises an eyebrow.

"You don't give a fuck about those pricks. We turn business away all the time."

His jaw sets. He rolls his neck to each side, then slowly shakes his head. "Natalie will hate us. She used to get pissed when her friends tried to get my attention. Zoe was one of the few who didn't."

I let his comment sink in, curious if he has more to say. The hum of the refrigerator is the only sound.

"Are you willing to sacrifice what we have with Zoe to make Natalie happy?" I'll have to give him credit for being selfless of epic proportions if he is.

His lips are pursed, his nostrils flare, and he slowly nods. "I love Zoe. I love everything about our girl. Every time I think of my future, she's in it. Hell, if Natalie wasn't in the picture, I'd marry Zoe."

Relief sweeps through me that we're on the same page. I try calling Zoe again, and it goes straight to voicemail.

Nathan confesses, "I'm sorry. I've been a chicken shit. I hoped I got her pregnant so she couldn't back out."

"I'd say it's a shit move but I hoped the same. And she didn't ask us to wear condoms, so I figure we might have all been hoping fate would take its course."

"Want to call our sister?"

"Let's leave that up to Zoe."

"Then we better go find her."

We get in the car and Jayce is rushing to our house. I roll my window down. "Now's not a good time."

He holds out a phone. "I found this. She must have set it down on my deck. I'm guessing you haven't been able to reach her."

Taking the phone from him, I'm ecstatic to have a piece of her in my possession, but at the same time, I worry that if she got into trouble, she couldn't reach us. Urgency flashes through me.

"Thanks, we're on our way to find her. And it's possible a marriage proposal will be on the table."

Jayce laughs. "Umm… She was pretty freaked out. Why don't you find out what's bothering her first."

I point at him. "You're a fucking genius. Thanks, man."

"Good luck."

"Let's not mention the marriage thing to anyone else until we've told her." Nathan offers the voice of reason.

"Got it. I'll rein it in."

Nathan rubs his temples while I drive. The winding road that will take us over the mountain and into town gives us time to plan.

He says, "She doesn't really talk about friends, and other than the grocery store, has only mentioned going to the bar."

I slam the heel of my hand on the steering wheel. "That's why she's pissed.

"Why?"

"We didn't let her do anything."

"You're right. Just like her parents. We even told her she shouldn't bartend."

"As if we should dictate what she does with her future."

"Fuck, we're assholes. Natalie's going to be pissed." Nathan brings up a valid point.

"Let's make this right."

"What if she needs more than we can offer?" Nathan's wise to consider everything.

"You said you love her."

"Yeah, and I would do anything for her. I'm ready to put it all on the line."

"We both are. I'm willing to fucking marry her right here right now."

The car is silent for a second and I can't believe that he's actually thinking. He needs to get out of his head.

"I was expecting more of a 'hell yeah' than silence. You just said you would marry her. I'm serious about wanting to fill her with babies."

"No, I wasn't doubting it. I'll marry her as soon as she'll let us, and you'll have to get in line for putting a baby in her. I was lost in a fucking daydream that we already got her pregnant. What if she freaked because she had a positive pregnancy test?"

I almost veer off the road. He's serious. I've never seen him look so happy.

He continues. "I can't go on without her. If it comes down to losing her or losing clients, I'll let the clients walk away every single time."

"That's a mother fucking plan." We high five and I take the curves a little faster.

"I've never been so screwed up. This seemed like the perfect arrangement. Our secret. We didn't have to deal with any of the hard stuff like how people would judge us. But when she said she quit, then ran to her car and drove away, it was like watching my life slip from my fingers."

He pounds his chest and takes a couple of breaths. "It's like I'm having a heart attack."

Crossing the mountain in record time, I drive straight to the Bottom Bar.

"She's here, but so are they." Nathan spies her car in the lot, one of the few vehicles that's not a motorcycle. The motorcycle club must all be there. Fan-fucking-tastic. They're big on protecting women. Can we catch a break?

"We have to be honest. I can feel it in my bones that this will work."

We stride in, immediately scanning the room for Goldie in the dim lighting. There's a rustle at the end of the bar and extra-thick bikers stand side by side.

They're intimidating in their own right, but nothing will stop us from getting to Goldie, not even the dirty dozen of other bikers who are watching us approach.

I hold my hands up. "We're looking for Goldie, um Zoe Simon. I think she might be behind you."

Rev, according to the name on the biker's vest, crosses his arms. "She asked not to be disturbed. Told us she quit her job today and could use a friend."

Anger rumbles through me but if I don't keep it under control, Nathan and I are no match for the gang. I'm determined, not stupid.

"Her bosses didn't get a chance to discuss her resignation."

I glance at Nathan and he says, "She didn't give them a chance to make things right."

The two men are planted firmly in place, their eyes steady on us. If not for the faint murmuring of Goldie's voice coming from behind them, I wouldn't be sure anyone heard us.

"That was on purpose." The biker relays.

My fingers twitch. I want to shove the two of them out of the way and have this conversation directly.

Regardless of how awkward it is to talk through these men, I keep the conversation going. "Come home so we can talk."

Barely a second elapses before Rev passes on, "Her mind is made up."

"Oh yeah?"

The silent biker, Torch, smirks. "You really can't take a hint."

"Our relationship is none of your fucking business."

"It is when a woman comes into our bar crying. Then a couple of pricks come in, acting like they own the place, and think they can tell her what to do." The coldness in his expression sends a shiver down my spine. This dude is intense.

She was crying? Fuck. My heart bottoms out.

This is going to be uncomfortable. I step closer to the men. They both widen their stances. I'm starting to think that out of all the places Goldie could choose to work, the bar might be the safest.

"You're right, we can't tell her what to do. And while I appreciate you standing up for her, she doesn't ever have to be afraid to tell us anything." I nod toward Nathan who's a step behind me.

"Then why'd she come in here with tears streaking her pretty face?"

"Because she doesn't know that we love her." As I said... Tell the truth.

"We do." Nathan interjects as I continue, "And the only thing that scares either of us more than how people will react to the three of us is missing the chance to find out."

Torch goes back to his silent judgment but it's with a smile this time. Rev huffs and nods before angling his head over his shoulder. "I think you should hear them out."

Did we just pass muster? My pulse pounds in my ears. Tunnel vision narrows to tiny fingertips poking between the arms of the biker barricade. Her fingers pry forward, pushing the guys apart. They make way for our little princess, the star of our happily ever after, and jealousy bangs around inside of me as she's guarded on either side by these two bikers.

"Love me?" The smallness in her voice draws me to step forward but Rev puts a hand up.

"We know it's hard to believe, but we're willing to risk everything for you. If our clients don't like our arrangement they can leave."

Nathan adds, "They accept all of us or none. We're a package deal. Not only do we want you in our lives, but you were also a freaking genius with the design idea. We want to hire you."

Rev grumbles over Goldie's squee.

"Hire me? Really?"

"Yeah, I actually told the client that our partner came up with the idea."

The bartender, Mammoth pats the wooden bar top, drawing Goldie's attention. "I love ya' too, all of us here do. I'll hire you tonight. With tips, I bet you'll make more money than with these stiffs."

I don't bother taking offense, but there's no way in hell I'll let him steal her away from us. My mouth opens to object but Torch gives me a curt nod and motions to Goldie.

She smiles sweetly at him then at the bartender. "Thanks, Mammoth. You guys are great, but there's no way you can pay better than them."

My entire world shifts as Goldie chooses us.

I can't hold back anymore. Nathan must have the same idea because we step forward at the same time. Snaking our arms around Zoe, we take back our missing piece.

Her temporary protectors step away. Nodding at them, I offer thanks for being there for her then scoop Goldie into my arms and carry her to the car.

Seventeen

Nathan

We leave Goldie's car at the bar and I give her the front seat while Carson drives us home.

She's no longer someone or something we'll keep hidden. We're ready to scream from the rooftop how much we love her, but we all agree to keep it quiet until we talk to Natalie.

My cock strains against my zipper as Carson's fingers tangle in Goldie's hair. His other hand stays firmly on the steering wheel as he navigates the switchbacks that carry us over the mountain.

It seems like I'm getting a reprieve when his hand slips from her hair. My erection backs off a touch, enough to take the edge off. But Carson doesn't return his hand to the steering wheel. I can't see where his fingers shift to, but Goldie's gasp gives me a damn good idea.

Fuck. I've never needed to nut so bad. Giving myself a firm grip, best I can through my jeans, I lean forward so I can see over the seat. She's spread wide. Carson's hand is tucked under her skirt which has ridden up.

"Pull your skirt up higher." My lips brush her ear. I need to see what he's doing.

With both hands, she bunches her skirt, balling it into one hand. Her face turns to mine but I'm staring down. "Is this better?"

Carson pumps his fingers in and out of her wet pussy, the erotic sound of her juices coating him threatens to push me over the edge. I'm losing my grip on sanity. Carson will never let me hear the end of it if I come in the backseat.

"You make everything better?" I grab her chin and crash my lips onto hers. The awkward strain of our over-the-seat kiss is putting even more pressure on my cock.

Her kisses grow sloppy and her breaths between them are heightened. She reaches both of her hands up, one grabbing my shoulder, the other lacing in my hair. I can't tell who's in control anymore. It's getting harder to hold back.

I plunge my tongue, fucking her mouth while Carson takes her closer to orgasm. Her entire body convulses, our kiss breaks, and she cries out while tightening her grip on me.

Shifting my hips just in time, I stave off my own release. I'm frantic. We're too far from home.

Carson alternates his gaze between the road and us. "We belong together."

Goldie's head lays heavily into mine as her climax fades.

Carson lifts his cum-soaked fingers, dragging his tongue over them. A lump forms in my throat. I can barely swallow. My tongue draws my lower lip in. "Give me a taste."

I don't know if he'll do it. Where is our line? We've never discussed it. Everything's been about Goldie.

His tongue pauses mid-swipe, then he sucks his fingers clean. I'm about to be pissed when he reaches down, drenching them in her release. Bringing them to my mouth, he lets me guide his fingers in. The thickness of his fingers coated in her intoxicating scent and her sweet taste fill a part of me I've never explored.

I have to disconnect or I'll lose control. Shifting back in my seat, I rub a hand over my cock. Diverting my gaze out the window, my huge exhale fogs the glass.

"You okay back there?" Carson glances over his shoulder, his eyes darting downward.

Adjusting my pants is no longer helpful. "Stop the car."

"Why?" he asks.

"I won't make it."

"Chill, we'll be home in a few minutes. We're not fucking on the side of the road."

"I'm getting in the front seat."

Goldie shifts in her seat and eyes me questioningly.

"You want me to jack you off too?" Carson asks.

I ignore him and drag my fingers under Goldie's chin. She's small enough, this could work. I'm running with an idea that I think her curious nature will love. "I want to sit you on my lap. Let me put a baby in you."

Carson growls, "She's still on the pill."

"I'll stop taking them."

Celebratory groans fill the car.

She bows her head to kiss my hand. "Why don't I just come back there?"

"I want Carson to be able to see you." I unbutton my pants.

"Like hell I'm going to chauffeur you two around while you fuck."

Goldie giggles. I love it when she does that. I love her excitement for life. I love her readiness to explore. She reminds me of all the things I don't do well and makes me want to be better, which is exactly why I've proposed this plan. In making her happy, we'll all be happy.

"If I'm on Nathan's lap, I could reach over here." She extends her arm and rubs Carson's thigh.

Suddenly, he's veering onto the slim shoulder of the road. We're on a short straightaway and there are no cars in sight. I hop out, lowering my zipper, shucking my clothes to my thighs as Goldie pops out, making room for me to sit.

"This is a really bad idea," Carson says but we maneuver into place.

There's barely room for the two of us so I grab my cock and hold it steady for her to sink onto. She's still soaked and swollen from her orgasm. My dick's never been wrapped so tight.

I grip her hips, easing her down my shaft until she's full of me. A few breaths help me stay focused.

Slamming the door, we forgo the seatbelt. "You better drive safe, we could be making a baby."

"Damn you, Nathan." Carson pulls onto the road.

"It'll be your turn next," she says, wrapping her fingers around his cock. He must have whipped it out when we were positioning. Apparently, the *really bad idea* isn't too upsetting.

"Fuck." His word is drawn out over a long breath as Goldie swipes the pre-cum from his tip and trails it down his shaft.

My fingertips dig into her hips as I pump her up and down while rocking my hips. I watch her stroke Carson while her pussy has a stranglehold on my cock.

The head of his dick strains and white pre-cum spills out with each stroke. The guy's as loaded and ready as I am.

"Taste him," I say.

Goldie raises her eyes to meet Carson's. There's a pause before he nods.

She loads her fingertip with the newest bead and angles it to her mouth. I catch the musky scent as she teases her fingertip over her tongue.

"That's so fucking hot." Goldie savors his essence while we slow fuck.

"Yeah, well my dick's getting cold over here." Carson's stroking his own cock. The head is redder and swollen.

SYLVIE HAAS

Goldie's shoulders raise and she withdraws her finger. Her small hand rests on his for a second before he switches positions with her, closing his big paw over her dainty one.

I lean Goldie into me, securing an arm around her waist, so I can kiss her neck and watch her stroke Carson at the same time.

"You like it when I show you how to stroke me?" Carson asks. She nods. "You're so hard. Does it hurt?"

"It hurts like hell, baby…knowing that you're riding Nathan's cock. You better be ready for me next because as soon as we get home, my dick gets a turn."

Her walls clamp around me and a mewl pours from her lips. Another pulse of her pussy around my cock. Shit. Her head falls back as she cries out her release.

I hold on to the last shred of control, but lose my grip when cum shoots from Carson's tip onto the steering wheel, his shirt, Goldie's hand, his pants…it's everywhere.

For a split second, I check to make sure his eyes are still on the road. He's good. Then I pump hard, letting go. My balls throw a Hail Mary, tightening so hard and fast, I don't have time to regroup.

My orgasm explodes into her. My growl reverberates through the car.

She's mine. My seed coats her womb. I will breed her if I haven't already, and if not this time, the next.

When we're spent, I loosen my grip and rub my hand on her belly. "Hope you're ready."

238

She rests her hand on mine. "I can't get pregnant yet."

"Don't be so sure."

Carson pulls into the garage, moves the seat back as far as it can go, and grabs her hands. "I warned you."

We both look down, and sure enough, his cum-covered cock is ready to go again. With a little maneuvering, we spin Goldie around so she's facing him and straddles his lap.

"If he didn't already do the job, I'm about to. And if he did, get ready for twins."

He hoists her over his tip, and I catch my breath as he slides her down. I push the button to close the garage door.

Goldie's able to work herself on his shaft. Her titties bounce and beg to be let free from her dress but this one doesn't have a zipper or buttons, damn it.

I lean over the center console, cradle her breast in my hand, and suck it into my mouth, cotton dress and all. I tease her nipple with my tongue. There's no doubt she can feel everything I'm doing as she moans with each flick.

Escalated breaths, fingers yanking my hair, and high-pitched begging come seconds before Carson slams into her. "Fuck!"

Their bodies tighten around me. I ease off her breast and watch the two of them release. This car's never going to smell the same again.

The next few days fly past. Zoe made us agree to get our work done before we play each day. Although, mid-morning break, lunch, and afternoon break are all viable times to sneak in a few orgasms for our new business partner.

Before we know it, I'm at the deck rail watching Natalie's car round the bend into the neighborhood. My stomach knots. I have to stop myself from biting my fingernail so I can offer a last-minute suggestion. "Maybe we should do shots before telling her."

Carson gets up, but Zoe grabs his hand. She says, "No. I don't want this to seem cheap or alcohol driven. We tell Natalie straight up."

"Okay, but I'll have shots ready for after we tell her."

She drops his hand. "Fair enough."

He disappears inside.

"I'll be right back. I have to nervous pee one last time." Zoe rushes inside.

Why does Natalie park at Lincoln and Jefferson's house? Lincoln's her boss, but even if she had to do a work thing, wouldn't she park here?

I step back from the railing, about to vomit. If she flips out...if she's mad at us and Zoe...if this whole thing comes crashing down into a fit of judgment and hurt, will Zoe still consider our relationship worthwhile?

Voices from below cause me to return to the railing. Lincoln is at her car talking to her. They need to handle business later.

Why the fuck is he brushing hair out of her face? And why is she laughing like a schoolgirl whose crush is giving her attention?

Her short shorts and crop top are not workplace appropriate, in fact, I've never seen her wear so little.

My overprotective brother mode flares into high gear. She's always so polite, never telling anyone to fuck off.

He's hitting on my little sister. She's his administrative assistant. What the fuck is wrong with him? Did we get her a job with a player?

He puts his hand on her lower back. Come on Natalie, tell him to knock it off. He's your boss.

Biting my tongue, I struggle to keep quiet. Natalie hates it when I *baby sister* her. Inching backward should help because I can't see them as well, but I just stare through the railing.

Am I in denial of what I'm seeing? Treating Natalie like a grown woman is important if I want Zoe treated like one. I have to trust her.

I turn away.

It works for a minute. Zoe and Carson return to the deck, reminding me of the need to reveal our relationship.

Playful, flirty laughter filters up to us. I visualize my identical neighbors using their charms on my little sister and my nausea returns. I spin around.

They're standing face to face, way too close. One of them—I can't tell which—has his fingers wrapped around her wrist, pinning it behind her back. He lowers his head, placing his lips next to her ear.

More flirty laughter. My fists ball. That sound isn't supposed to come from my sister.

Zoe chuckles. She and Carson join me at the rail.

"Looks like Natalie found some friends." Zoe laughs.

Not funny. "One of them is her boss."

"Oh, a workplace romance!"

"He might be taking advantage of her," I defend.

"Is it your call to make?" Zoe nudges an elbow into my side.

Fuck, she's right. Not just because I want to protect Natalie. Not just because I respect that she gets to make her own choices. This could be a relevant talking point.

Time to be a big brother and set a good example.

Natalie turns. I think everything will be okay, then he swats her ass. If her grin wasn't huge, if she didn't turn and wave her finger at him playfully, I might not be losing my mind.

But all of that happened, and I am.

"Christ man, you don't look so good." Carson guides me to a chair.

I sit, my elbows on my knees, and fist my hair on both sides of my head. I can do this.

They keep me calm for the few minutes Natalie and her boss and his twin are doing god knows what. The click of the downstairs door, a pause, then the sound of them coming up the steps has me taking deep breaths.

"Holy crap, bro, are you sick?" Natalie's quick to get to the point but I'm relieved that she's alone.

I've failed to come up with a casual way to bring up our ménage. Pulling my shit together, I motion for her to have a seat. Carson and Zoe follow suit.

"I'll be a lot better once we talk."

She holds a finger up to me. "If you're going to lecture me about what you just saw, stop right now."

"That's part of what I wanted to talk about. But I won't lecture you, even though he's a...never mind, no lecture...what did I see?"

"Not sure yet. I've had a thing for Lincoln since my first day on the job. Then I met his twin and we all clicked.

"Fuck, Natalie, he's old enough—"

"Nathan!" Natalie scolds.

Carson and Zoe crack up. I'm not handling this well.

"What Nathan's trying to say is that he respects your decisions, and hopes you'll respect ours too." Zoe's statement is bold. I hope not too much so. This isn't exactly easing Natalie into the idea.

I can see Nat's wheels turning as she shifts her gaze to each of us. "Ours? As in you three?"

"All three of us. It just kind of happened. We were worried it would upset you, but Natalie, we'd love to have your blessing."

The pause is long enough, I wonder if my sister's gone catatonic. She's upright and looks normal but remains emotionless.

I give it a go. "Natalie, we tried to deny it. We didn't want to put you in a weird spot, but it's the best thing I've ever done."

She recovers from her stupor. "Wow." Nat shifts her attention to Zoe. "Have you always been attracted to Nathan?"

Zoe purses her lips and nods. "I'm sorry. I should have turned the cleaning job down when I realized it was your brother's house."

Natalie rubs her hands over her eyes. "Cleaning isn't exactly the problem. You have to work. But geez, Zoe... All those years you sat silently while I bitched about girls falling all over themselves for my brother."

"You were more important to me. And it's not that you aren't important to me now, but I've never felt this way for any other guy." She looks from me to Carson. "Guys."

Natalie scrunches her face. "Okay, as long as all of you promise not to gross me out, and Nathan double promises not to interfere with me and the neighbors, I'll try to understand...and no best friend chats about your boyfriends anymore."

"Deal." We all say it at the same time.

"Do you mind if I go let Lincoln and Jefferson know that you're okay with this?"

"I wouldn't say I'm okay," I say defensively.

"Nathan. No interfering." Natalie flashes me a look that reminds me too much of the stern look our mom gave when she had to call us out on stupid shit.

"Fine. But if either of them hurts you..."

"You'll be the first to know. I promise." She jumps up, hugs me, Zoe, then Carson then rushes out.

I pull Zoe onto my lap, but it's not until I brush the hair from her face that I see she's crying. "What's wrong?"

I wipe the tears away with my thumbs and Carson sits beside us.

"I didn't think this would happen. It's a dream come true." She snuggles in tighter, finding out that I'm sporting an erection.

"You're the dream come true, Goldie. And I'll spend the rest of my life making sure you have your happily ever after. I love you more than anything." I slide a hand between her legs and circle her clit through her shorts.

She shudders. "I love you too, both of you."

Carson leans in, his forehead bridging ours, inches apart. "I love you too."

I drop my head to the other side of Goldie's neck. I have to focus on rewarding her with an orgasm for helping us come clean about our relationship. Carson takes advantage of my move and claims her mouth.

We're perfect together. And I have a feeling we're about to be even better.

Epilogue

Zoe

Four years later

Stretching as I resist waking up, I sense the weight of someone watching me. Our little girl is next door with Aunt Natalie and her kids, which is why I have the luxury of lounging on the rooftop deck.

I'm on my back with my arms overhead, wrists overlapping, pretending I'm still asleep. If I was anywhere other than our private deck, I'd be worried who's silently watching me.

It's such a far cry from four years ago when I'd awoken with a startle when Carson and Nathan caught me sunbathing. This time I really do have a bathing suit on, but it doesn't cover any more than my bra and panties did that day. The rooftop deck is still my favorite place to relax, and the majesty of the mountains surrounding us never grows old.

Shifting my hips, I thrust my ass the direction I can tell the guys are watching from. I let out a tiny moan.

Lower, more gravelly moans confirm both guys are there.

I keep my breaths calm, my expression relaxed. I love letting them look at me. They always have so much adoration in their eyes, unless of course, it's replaced by feral, primal, immediate need.

I'm still their adventurous Goldilocks who likes to try new things so I try out the fake sleep thing.

If they're horny, which I'm sure they are, they're getting rock hard.

The hurried clicks of a zipper lowering, followed by clothes hitting the ground validate my assessment.

I wait. My head is turned away, helping my efforts to suppress a smile.

"What do we have here? Is someone sleeping on our roof?" Nathan says playfully.

"I don't think she's sleeping. I think she's waiting."

"What do you suppose she's waiting for?"

The firm padding of footsteps stops on either side of me. A large hand grips my wrists. Carson. A shiver wiggles down my spine. They know I'm awake, but we have fun playing.

"I bet she wants you to come on her tits, Nathan." Carson's jacking himself off beside my face, best I can tell from the fapping sound.

"Is that so?"

"Yeah, because I'm going to be inside of her pussy, and she won't want you to be left out."

I snicker and remain uselessly still, not wanting to sneak a peek lest I spoil the moment.

"We'll see about that."

Carson's strokes stop and his hand slides over my belly, which he's obsessed with even when I'm not pregnant. His fingers stop at the top of my bikini bottom.

Damn him. I squeeze my thighs together.

Nathan tugs my wrists a little higher. He wants me exposed, and I love making them happy. Neither of them cares that my belly's not as flat as it used to be. They've been trying to put another baby in it, anyway. Little do they know I'm planning on telling them my little secret today. That's why I sent our cutie pie daughter to Natalie's.

Carson says, "You need some lube before waking her up?" His hand slips into my suit. "I bet she's got some lube handy for us."

"Yeah, her sweet cream is the best."

My sex tingles and hints of an orgasm knot in my core. Carson drags his finger back and forth through my curls. What's he going to do? Will he smear my juices on his brother's cock? I peek. Nope. Just on his hand.

Staying still is becoming nearly impossible as I need him an inch or so lower so I can ride his hand. Or Carson needs to make good on getting his big fat cock inside of me.

But they're enjoying this as much as I am so I find the strength to delay my pleasure.

He dips his fingers lower, avoiding my clit, motherfucker, but I like where this is going.

Nathan adds his fingers to my sopping wet...lube. I arch my back a little, forcing his hand to touch my clit.

My legs reflexively tighten around them but Nathan gets free and strokes his cock .

"We better hurry. I think she's about to wake up." Carson pulls his hand away.

"I'm so ready." Nathan's grip tightens around my wrists. I'm about to open my eyes but I don't hear the strokes anymore.

"Hang on. Let me get a little more." Nathan's hand is on my sex, this time the heel of his hand presses into my clit while he coats his fingers. If he keeps going much longer, I'm going to blow my ruse, and probably squirt. Guess he'll be plenty wet if that happens.

"Do you suppose an orgasm would wake our sleeping beauty?" Nathan says, his fingers making mind-blowing circles of my clit.

My body lurches and I'm about to lose control when he lifts his hand. Damn it, he loves leaving me hanging, only because he knows it gets me even hotter.

"I don't know about sleeping beauty, but we have Goldilocks. The way I hear it, she likes trying different things." Carson's voice hitches for the last few words and the sound of a cock being stroked by a very wet hand resumes.

"What should we try today? Daytime sex on the rooftop?"

"I'm pretty sure you're doing it." Carson can barely talk. He must be stroking himself again. Not to be picky, but he said he was going to put his dick in me and I'm more than ready.

I pop an eye open. The thoughts I had of asking for a special wake-up kiss on my clit dissipate. Nathan's thick cock drips pre-cum into my hair.

They're completely naked, but with the low wall around the deck, no one can see anything that matters.

Nathan's hand continues to grip me as he resumes stroking himself.

I cross my legs, desperate to ease the tension in my core. I try to tug a hand free but Nathan grips harder and smiles down at me.

"Somebody's watching us, Carson."

He looks down at me, slowing his strokes. "Don't move."

The intensity of his demand rips through me, pushing me to the brink.

"Don't you dare make yourself come. I want you to be desperate for my cock." Carson's not usually one for making me wait. Hopefully, that means he's about to fuck me.

"Uncross your legs." Nathan gently slaps my pussy when I don't immediately comply. "Be a good girl and do what you're told."

The only way I can keep from squeezing my thighs together is to drop my legs on either side of the chair. If anything, me being spread should hurry them along.

"Look at that, our dirty girl is spread and ready. Are you going to behave and leave your hands up here?" Nathan asks.

"Yes." I can't play coy or think of anything sexy to say with their erections looming over me.

Nathan releases my wrists and I desperately want to touch myself but I don't have to. His hand is on my bathing suit, pressing the wet fabric into me. His smile widens with each flinch of my hips.

"I think you liked teasing us by pretending to be asleep."

"I like giving up control to you."

His fingers tuck under my suit.

"Do you need to come?"

"Yes." I wiggle into him but he won't let me get off.

"You like watching us touch ourselves?"

"It's so hot."

"I think you're wet enough we don't need to get the lube. If you promise not to come, we'll jerk off with your juices. You want us to do that?"

"I don't know if I can stop myself."

"I know you can, but will you?" Nathan flicks the tip of his finger over my clit and Carson stares down at me and says reassuringly, "It makes me extra hard knowing you need to come. Do it for me."

"I'll do it." I pant through the intermittent passes over my clit and into my pussy Nathan's giving me.

"That's my girl." Carson strokes his fingers through my hair.

"I want it too."

Carson pulls his hand away and Nathan drags his back through my wetter-by-the-minute sex.

Nathan stares me in the eyes. "This is for you."

"Put your hands back up or we'll stop," Carson growls.

I hadn't even realized I was lowering my arms. Sliding them back into place, I grab the top of the chair and squeeze my legs against the wooden sides.

"Please hurry."

They're stroking themselves, hips moving in sync. I writhe underneath them, loving the intimacy but desperate to be touched. Then I am.

Nathan ejaculates first. The first spray hits Carson's cock and Nathan's own hand. That triggers Carson and they're both shooting their loads. They angle themselves to get more of it on me, and I love it, their hot streams combining to make one big mess.

But if I can't move my hands soon, they better get busy because I need to come.

I fake pout.

Carson catches my disappointment. "I guess you're ready for your turn."

"You said Nathan was going to come on my chest while you filled my pussy."

"Don't worry Goldie, I'm headed there now." Carson slides my bikini bottom off.

"But you just..." I drag a hand over their mixed release.

"I'm still hard thinking about how badly you need to come right now. I had this special feeling about today. I might be crazy, but I think it's my turn to get you pregnant." His tip slides over my clit, sending a shiver through my body before he repositions and spreads my needy lips.

"Nope."

"What? I thought you wanted us to knock you up again." He pumps into me. "Now's not a good time to change your mind."

"I didn't change my mind."

Nathan slows his strokes and gives me a confused look.

"There's already a baby in there."

"Fuck, yeah!" Carson's cock throbs.

My orgasm is like a starburst of energy, fueled by his thrusts as my fingernails dig into Carson's back. I hold on for dear life as his cock swells, filling me with cum that won't get to do its job. Nathan's release is just as useless on my face, other than reminding me just how crazy these guys are for me.

Then Nathan uses his shirt to wipe my face, and they slide chairs next to mine. We snuggle under the midday sun. Their love for me is so intense, sometimes I wonder if I'm lost in one of those heat fantasies.

I peek an eye open to confirm this is real and thank a coffee spill for making me the luckiest girl on the planet.

And we live happily ever after!

A bonus scene for this story is available exclusively to newsletter subscribers. Want to know if Nathan and Carson only use the pool table for crafting strategic shots? Grab this bonus scene to find out!

Sign up at: https://www.SylvieHaas.com And true to my initials, SHhhh, I'll let it be our little secret.

Claimed by my Lawyers

A Ménage Romance

Part of the
Eggplant Canyon series

Sylvie Haas

Blurb

My lawyers make being naughty feel good!

When a high-powered lawyer and his intern not only want to take my case but insist that I'm their girlfriend, I think I'm dreaming.

But I'm not. And they're serious. They want me to be theirs in every way.

Can they protect me from a courtroom reveal about our relationship? Or will I end up locked up and pregnant?

If you love dirty-talking men who have over-the-top ideas of how to please their woman and want to give her babies, you'll want these guys coming to your defense!

One

The stress lines etched across Public Defender Frank Wallace's forehead fail to put me at ease. The off-white walls of the overly small conference room that could hold four people max, isn't exactly the shining backdrop of confidence.

"The burden is on the accuser to prove you were negligent," he assures me.

There has to be more I can do than hope the prosecution fails. Diverting my gaze to the thin vertical window in the door, my breath catches at the sight of a sinfully handsome man who stopped in the hallway and is staring at me.

Our eyes lock, and I'm swept away from my problems.

"Miss Solis?" Frank clears his throat.

"Call me Yvette." The breathiness of my statement hits my ears. I'm not sure if I'm saying it to Frank or the man in the hallway, who I can't tear my gaze from.

I'm not ready to drift back to the cold, hard reality where I'm being sued by a customer who suffered anaphylactic shock while eating a donut in my barely-making-a-profit, peanut-free bakery. I still can't figure out how it happened.

I'd rather stay lost in this stranger's eyes, imagining a world where he'll sweep me off my feet, sequester me in his mansion, and teach me about sexual needs I didn't know I had. And if he could erase my legal woes, that would be a bonus.

That would be kidnapping. Wrong on so many levels. Unless of course, I didn't object.

I'd like to choose door number one, please. Not the time for humor. Not the time to reconsider my life choices of putting my business success above dating. Not that a man like the guy in the hallway, who exudes wealth and power, would be interested in a simple-life-loving bakery owner.

"Sorry." I force my attention away from the perfectly groomed and tailored man beyond the door, back to the kind soul across the table.

The possessive gaze from the hallway still weighs on me. Does the stranger feel the same attraction I do?

I'm such an idiot. I bet he assumes the defendants stuck in this room are guilty, poor, or both. My stomach sinks.

Am I guilty? No.

Am I negligent? Impossible.

Am I poor? I would be okay living off love.

Frank's voice raises. "Miss Solis. Please focus. I only have the room reserved for a few more minutes. With the holidays coming up, it's going to be harder to get in touch with people.

Our time is limited. You need to gather information from your vendors stating their nut-free policies. If Nurse Aria hadn't been in your bakery, Mister Benedict might have died. You have to take this seriously."

"You think I don't take this seriously? My bakery exists to give people with nut allergies a safe place to enjoy pastries." The lump in my throat refuses to back down. Tears threaten. Anger takes over. "When I was seventeen, I held my little sister in my lap after jamming an epi-pen into her thigh and watched for any sign of life. I'd snuck her out of the house for a donut, thinking she was being deprived of one of the greatest pleasures on earth. My teenage cockiness and ignorance almost killed her. I triple-check food safety with each of my vendors and require my employees to watch a video on anaphylactic shock."

Frank smiles and nods. "Good."

"What?" I break. Tears stream down my face.

"That's the story we need when you're on the stand. Tear out the hearts of every jury member. And get me a copy of your employee—"

A whoosh of air hits me as the door flies open. Frank jerks back in his chair, and I whip my head to see who barged in.

The form-fitting navy-blue suit, the intricate paisley pattern of the silk tie that matches the pocket square, and the starched white shirt spanned over a broad, muscular chest delay the drag of my eyes to Mister Sinfully Possessive's face.

He steps closer, forcing me to crane my neck as he towers over me. I can't breathe. Has he consumed all of the oxygen in the room, or is my neck at a funny angle? Or maybe I am struggling to breathe because his rich, musky cologne infuses my core.

My sex tingles, as does every inch of my skin. I wish he would close the small gap between us and scoop me up. I'm ready.

"What's going on?" a deep voice calls from immediately behind him. Time slows. Hopefully, the minuscule pause can be played off as surprise.

"Frank made our girlfriend cry."

"Who?" the man in back asks as he squeezes himself into the room.

Good question. I sort the pieces one at a time. Okay, Mister Possessive and my public defender know each other. Mister Possessive must have me mistaken for someone else. That would explain why he stared at me. But even more intriguing is that he said, "*Our* girlfriend."

The tingling roars into a full-blown craving. *Please, please, please, whisk me away.* I haven't seen the other guy yet. I don't care.

The man in back steps to where he can see me. "Oh."

I'm swept away by his piercing green eyes and youthful vigor contrasted against Mister Possessive's dominant confidence. The world stops. Do I look that much like their girlfriend? Or does he see through me?

I think I'm swooning. He's every bit as pulled together but probably a decade younger, only a few years older than me. Where were guys like this in my high school?

His gaze narrows as it shifts from me to the first man.

I open my mouth, but Possessive puts a finger to my lips. "It's okay, baby girl. You should have told me you were in trouble."

The thick pad of his finger drags over my lower lip. A flicker of confusion flashes over the younger man's face but he quickly steels his expression. I wish I could do the same.

Letting Possessive believe I'm his baby girl is the most tempting thing I've ever faced. But fraud on top of negligence would only make things worse. Besides, as soon as I open my mouth, they won't recognize my voice.

I take the high road like always. "I'm..."

Why can't I force the words out?

"Shh. We'll take care of you. Why don't you give us the room, Frank." Not a question. His command is intoxicating.

Frank stands.

"You can't just barge in here, Hendrix. I'm meeting with a client."

My heart slams against my rib cage. Hendrix Morgan? The esteemed, reclusive lawyer? He only takes high-end clients and almost always settles out of court. No wonder the younger man lets him lead.

I mentally check myself. That's a big assumption based on a first name.

Hendrix nods at Frank. "*Your* client is *our* girlfriend."

No matter how much I'd like this to be true—and I'd willingly let this pair of men do whatever they want to me—I pull myself from my lust-addled brain. Whatever the connection I thought I felt when our eyes first met was clearly mistaken identity. And yet, I still can't force words out of my mouth.

"Merry Christmas, Frank, I'm taking over her representation. One less case for you to worry about." Hendrix's gaze instantly softens as he shifts it from Frank to me. "I'll need you to give your consent. Will you do that for me, baby?"

His eyes bore into me—willing me to obey.

Yes is about to tumble from my lips. But once he finds out I'm not who he thinks he is, he'll drop my case, won't he? Then I won't have a regular lawyer or a public defender. Embarrassing this guy doesn't seem like a wise move either. I motion with my finger for him to lean down.

That was a bad decision. He doesn't lean. He kneels, resting one hand on my thigh, which sends repeated jolts of electricity to my sex. I might come from that alone. But it's when his other finger lifts a lock of my hair and the back of his hand gently brushes the top of my breast that I moan.

Good heavens, what is wrong with me?

One glance at Frank slams me back into my dire situation.

I lean toward Hendrix's ear, barely stopping myself before making contact. I whisper, "You have me mistaken. I'm not your girlfriend. I'm Yvette Solis."

He leans away. "Baby, Yvette... It's okay to let Frank know about our relationship." Hendrix nods over his shoulder to include the other man with whom I'm apparently in a relationship.

Is he insane?

Am I being pranked?

When he turns back to me, he leans so close that his breath coats my lips. His eyes pierce mine. Is he going to—?

I'm paralyzed as his lips brush over mine. He takes more, breaking me free. I kiss him back. I'm whoever he wants me to be. I'm his.

And he's gone. His lips are anyway. A smile lightens his face as he continues. "Frank is bound by attorney-client privilege. He can't tell anyone about us. All you have to do is let Frank know that you want your boyfriends to be your legal representatives."

I'm so confused. Why the hell would Hendrix Morgan insist on representing me? And that I'm his girlfriend?

"Do you have a business card?" It's the only way I can think to confirm he's the Hendrix I think he is.

He smirks, stands, letting his fingers slowly pull from my thigh, then retrieves a business card from the inside pocket of his suit jacket.

I take it from his fingers, careful not to touch him, for fear of melting. The card confirms that he's exactly who I think he is. Can I really be this lucky? It doesn't matter. Whatever he's up to, I'm grasping the crazy opportunity in front of me. And I hope the girlfriend angle can be more than a ruse.

Smiling up at him then at the younger guy, I can't believe what I'm about to do. I slide the business card across the table and say, "Mister Wallace, thank you for your help. I'd like to accept Mister Morgan's...my boyfriend's offer to be my legal representative from here on out."

While I'm saying things I don't understand, I notice Hendrix motioning for the younger man to give me his business card. "Here you go, love."

Love? This is more awkward by the moment. O*ur girlfriend* must have been deliberate.

I read his name from the card and note that he's an intern, before offering the card to Frank. "Damian Weatherford..." I swallow hard. "My other boyfriend, will be assisting."

When no one bursts through the door announcing the prank, I look at the ceiling, which has a skylight. Blue skies overhead show no signs of lightning striking me. So far, there's no punishment for my lie.

"Now, Frank... Would you kindly let us have the room with our client?" Hendrix phrases it as a question this time, and somehow, it's even more powerful.

My heart flutters as Frank nods at me. His furrowed brow betrays his respectful tone. "I don't know what just happened, but you're in good hands."

Two

I'm breathless as the two men shuffle around me to make room for Frank to exit. What have I done...aside from lying to my public defender and kicking him off my case? My *free* public defender. How did I manage to forget that before firing him? I sink into my chair.

Would I seriously consider paying Hendrix and Damian with sex? And since when did I become so confident in my desirability and sexual prowess?

The tension in the air should be related to the charges against me, but I'm shamefully more interested in the girlfriend proposition. I clasp my hands in my lap and lower my head. I don't want them to see the blush I can feel taking over my cheeks.

Damian closes and locks the door. "I know you're up to something, but you'll have to let me in on it, boss."

I peek up at them. Hendrix nods at Damian then kneels in front of me. I'd love for this to be my new normal, but I'm not delusional. Not usually.

Damian sits on the end of the table, angling himself toward us.

Hendrix places his hand on mine. "I'm sure that left you confused too, but it was the only way to handle it. Allow me to explain."

Before I embarrass myself, I take a deep breath and raise my head with some sense of reality. "Yes, please explain why you convinced me to fire my free legal counsel. I can't afford your rates."

The obvious option, which I'm trying to deny might exist—that Hendrix might have used the girlfriend line to suggest payment in sex—has my sex simmering greedily. I wish I could say I'm above that. But if it's what we all want, why not?

That damn connection that has been present for all of the ten minutes or so I've known him is stronger than ever. And it's from him *and* Damian. I've never felt something so protective, like I belong to them.

Surprisingly, I don't shudder at the sensation. I also don't offer myself just yet. This is happening too fast.

"Pay very close attention to the timeline." Hendrix pauses.

"Okay."

"Damian and I came in. The three of us agreed that you're our girlfriend. Only after that did you hire us as your legal counsel."

I shrug. His order of events is factually correct.

Damian jumps in. "Fucking genius. I hadn't known where you were going with that at first, Hendrix, but I get it. We can't initiate a romantic relationship with a client, but if that relationship exists prior to being retained as counsel, it's permissible."

"Of course, we'll waive our fees for our girlfriend," Hendrix adds.

"Thank you," I say. "If you ever need something sweet, I'm your girl."

Hendrix's eyes go dark. "Yes, you are."

Damian shifts uneasily.

"Oh! I meant food, donuts, and other pastries. I own a bakery."

"Hmm."

I don't know what to make of Hendrix's response. I also need more help. "I'm confused. Why take the case? You don't even know if I'm guilty, or what the charges are." I take a deep breath. "Or if you'd want me as your girlfriend."

His big hand squeezes mine. "Baby, the second I saw you, I had to have you."

"I felt the same way." Why do I say that? Sure, I wanted him to kidnap me... Okay, I did feel the same way. I just didn't consider it possible. And I had bigger issues, which I still have, but they seem so much smaller now.

"The way we connected through that tiny glass window, I sensed my future."

My entire world just got tossed into my big dough mixer. Nothing feels normal anymore. I look at Damian, desperate for him to say yes. "What about you?"

Damian drags a hand over the back of my head and grips my hair, tilting my head up. His lips crash onto mine. I willingly open for him, and he takes what I offer.

"Enough," Hendrix growls.

The hierarchy I'd suspected plays out.

As Damian steps back, he says, "I didn't see you until we were inside the room, but my fucking heart stopped. If you hadn't agreed to be our girlfriend, I might have died."

I nod as Hendrix lowers his hand to my thigh. His thumb easily reaches down, caressing between my legs as much as my skirt will allow. I'd thought I needed to look professional for the lawyer to take me seriously. Normally I'm a sundress and flip-flops kind of girl.

"Will we get in trouble?" My breaths grow heavy.

"Not since you're a good girl and agreed to be our girlfriend." Hendrix moves both of his hands to my knees, allowing his fingers to dabble at the hem of my skirt.

The way he says *good girl* is so vastly different than the good girl I've always considered myself. My panties are soaked. But my kind of good girl would have never taken this offer. She'd play it safe. That's gotten her nowhere.

The good girl that agreed to be their girlfriend? I'm glad they introduced me to her. She could have a lot of fun and would have been either of their girlfriends, no strings attached.

Gentle pressure guides my knees apart. My skirt sags between them, allowing me a touch of decency that I'm not sure I want.

They are what I want.

A knock on the door kills the moment. Panic consumes me. Hendrix's firm grip on my knees won't let me close them. Damian is already up, covering the window with his buff, oversized body.

"I have the room scheduled right now," a muffled voice says through the door.

"Sorry, our client is in distress. Our debriefing is going to run long. Find another room."

There's a brief exchange between the two, but I lose track of it as Hendrix moves a hand under my skirt. A million questions threaten, like what if the scheduled person comes back with a key. Hendrix's hands are around my hips. He pulls me so that my ass is on the edge of the chair.

"Be a good intern, Damian, and keep that door closed."

"Anything to protect her."

Protect me?

"You ready to be ours?" Hendrix asks.

"Yes." This is happening, and more importantly, I want it to. I played it safe my whole life, except for taking my sister to the donut shop, then went right back to being a good girl. What's the catch? Why do these wealthy, powerful men want me?

I can't escape the obvious. Might as well try to take advantage of it and fall into the role. "Are you ready for your payment?"

Hendrix's eyes go wide and his hand stills. Damian chokes on my statement, perhaps as surprised by my sexy voice as I am. They both look hungry, ready to pounce. Damian's cock strains against his slacks. His need eggs me on. How can I be so vulnerable and so strong at the same time?

"This isn't payment." Hendrix's tone is firm.

Well, crap. Only I could biff this kind of offer. "But I thought..."

"Our legal services are free. This..." His thumbs caress the insides of my thighs while his hands are planted firmly on top. "This is because you're ours, and I need to get you ready before I make love to you." He moves the caresses up to my panties, making it far too clear that he now knows how wet I am.

His groan kicks my need into high gear.

Damian says, "Unless you want to pretend that you owe us. We can make sure you pay in full."

"Yes."

"Fuck. You're a naughty girl," Hendrix says almost reverently.

"That's why I need a good lawyer to protect me." I don't know where my bravado is coming from, but I'm running with it.

He grips harder.

"Get her skirt out of the way. She owes me too." Damian says.

Not wanting Hendrix to let go of me, I lift my skirt and ball it against my chest. "Like that?"

Hendrix lunges forward, pinning my hands against my body, kissing me, plunging his tongue between my lips. Need pings back and forth between my mouth and his thumb circling my clit. Then he pulls away and dives down, lapping at my center, his tongue dragging over my panties. I gasp at the sudden contact. If I dared to move, I'd rip my panties off. But I can't. I don't dare miss a second of his expertise. Cries of pleasure keep me from catching my breath.

Damian lifts his finger to his lips. "Shh. Be a good girl and keep quiet, or those sexy sounds will have all the lawyers lined up at the door offering to help."

I bite my lips while Hendrix finds my clit through the fabric and flicks the tip of his tongue over it. How can he do that? I've never gotten this close to climaxing this fast. I can't believe I'm going to come while we're all fully dressed. Is that the biggest surprise here?

"Does she taste as good as she smells?"

Can Damian really smell me? I should be embarrassed. His eyes are fixed on my lap. I don't know how much he can see with Hendrix's head there, but he looks entranced—eyes wide, mouth agape.

Hendrix pauses and looks over his shoulder, not even bothering to wipe my wetness from his face. "Even better."

The brief seconds of reprieve allow me to catch my breath.

"Mind if I give Damian a taste?" He slides a finger into my panties. Reprieve over.

Oh my god. Is he saying what I think he's saying? I've never had a threesome. I hadn't thought about the mechanics of it until the last few minutes. Hendrix pulls his finger out and holds it up for me to see. It glistens with my juices.

"He's being helpful standing guard. One little taste could be a retainer for his services."

I glance up at Damian, and he's licking his lips. His eyes have lifted from my spread-eagle position, even though he'd have a better view of my sex. He's watching my eyes. Waiting for my answer.

'I'd like that." I drop my gaze brazenly to his tented pants.

"Fuck," Hendrix mutters as he gets to his feet. He leans down and kisses my lips...gently at first, then his tongue slides into my mouth, and I surrender.

I'm panting when he pulls away. He strokes his finger inside my panties again, this time brushing between my pussy lips.

Have they done this before? Do I care? I watch with rapt attention and an ever-increasing need to climax as he steps toward Damian.

"You're not going to believe how good this is." He lifts his hand far too slowly.

Damian's mouth drops open. His chest rises and falls as he stares at my spread legs while waiting to be fed, or paid. I've always wanted to role-play.

This has to be a dream.

Hendrix dips his fingertips in Damian's mouth. I drop a hand to my sex, only partially aware that I've done it. The pain from my imminent orgasm is unbearable. I need relief. I need a cock in me. I need more of everything they're offering.

Then Damian leans forward, closing his mouth around Hendrix's fingers. It shatters me. My legs slam shut around my hand. I circle my clit in desperate motions, no longer offering slight relief, but plunging myself over the edge.

I stifle as much sound as I can. And when I catch enough of a coherent thought to realize what I've done, I lift my head from where I've dropped it backward. My eyes still closed and heavy with lust.

Wouldn't I have woken up if this was a dream? The weight of the room has changed dramatically.

Forcing my eyes open so I can figure out if I'm dreaming, I find Hendrix has stepped in front of me, his expression stern. Damian remains at the door.

It's not a dream. And yet it is.

Hendrix grips my upper arms and lifts me. "Did you just pay yourself?"

For a split second, I think he means *play* with yourself, then I snap back to the role-play. They don't know that I'm not like this. I pray that at the end of all of this, they're really going to help me with my case. "Am I not supposed to do that?"

"You have two lawyers who can't work for free."

"Sorry for being a naughty girl. I'll pay whatever you want." That might have gone too far. I'm not wildly experienced, but the sense of safety I have with them, which is the only reason I can do this, urges me forward.

"Bend over the table." Hendrix keeps his voice low.

Here? I'm stirred into a total frenzy. With Damian guarding the locked door, there's no chance we'll get caught, but I've only ever had sex in my bed. And only twice. And only missionary. And only with one guy. And I didn't climax.

I'm done being the wrong kind of good girl.

Hendrix slides my skirt over my bottom, leaving me exposed in a whole new way.

Damian says, "A thong? You wore a thong under this short skirt? You are a naughty girl."

Now I'm confused. Am I supposed to be a good girl or a naughty girl?

Hendrix rubs his hand over my bare ass cheek, squeezes a few times, then slaps it.

I flinch, and my sex tightens, desperately needing a cock to fill it. Why did I never feel like this with my boyfriend? I'm not dreaming, and this has gone way too far to be a prank. How the heck did I go from nearly killing a man to living a fantasy?

Hendrix rubs the sting away. "If we didn't have to be quiet, I'd slap it a lot harder."

"Save that for later, man." Damian implies this will continue. Where? They definitely can't come to my messy one-bedroom apartment.

The warmth of Hendrix's hand disappears. The sounds of a belt being loosened and a zipper dropping keep me from having to guess what he's doing.

I glance over my shoulder and can't decide if I'm excited or worried when I see the size of his cock. It's glorious in all its hugeness.

"Give me her panties," Damian demands.

Fingers hook into the slim waistband on either side of my hips. They slowly drag the fabric down, then it sounds like Damian catches them. I can't look. This is crazy. But with Hendrix on his knees again, this time behind me, I can't believe anything is off-limits.

His tongue against my pussy makes my legs weak. I drop my head onto my hands and accept the surge of the passion he creates.

"Damn, baby girl, are you getting close again?" His breath is hot against my sex. I clamp my eyes shut, forcing thoughts of sprinkle donuts into my mind so I can avoid imagining what he's looking at.

"Yes." How can this feel so right?

He bites my ass. I shudder. Didn't know I liked getting my ass bit.

There's a little bit of shuffling as he stands. Then his tip presses between my pussy lips. "I'm going to take you bare."

"But..." My statement falters. Why don't I want to object?

"How else am I going to ensure you're mine?" He presses in farther. "And give you my baby."

This is completely reckless. Completely enticing. Am I losing my mind?

Adjusting his stance, he fills me with another inch. It's already putting pressure on my clit as he stretches me. Sanity slips away.

Inch by inch, he pulses in and out of me, going farther every few thrusts. If this is how sex is supposed to feel, maybe I'm a virgin. Too late to discuss that. And too hard to explain my reasoning.

"Are you okay? You're tighter than I expected you to be."

"I'm okay."

"I'll give you a second."

"That good?" Damian's question draws my attention. I angle my head. His back remains against the door, but his eyes shift to mine as Hendrix responds with a groan. "Damn. I can't wait to sink into you, love." He runs with the nickname that for some reason sounds extra hot coming from a giant, mid-twenties piece of male perfection.

"I can't wait either."

But wow, Hendrix is a lot, and we haven't even done anything.

I push against him. His cock twitches, and the strength of his fingers digging into my hips warns me we're about to go for a wild ride.

His thrusts start slow and long. The dragging of his cock through me is the most amazing thing I've ever felt. A tinge of pain comes with the stretch, but it keeps my clit sensitive. Each movement drives me closer, creating a bigger buildup than I've been able to give myself.

And being watched. That's part of the turn-on. Both of them want me, and only one gets me right now.

Knock. Knock. Knock.

Why does that push me closer to orgasm? My walls tighten around his cock.

"We have a reservation system, and you'll need to relinquish the room to the person who's on the list."

Is it adrenaline? The fear of not finishing? It's the last straw. I thrust my ass against Hendrix, pushing myself into the orgasm, choking on every moan and cry that begs for release. My body shakes, and I take Hendrix with me.

I look over my shoulder in time to see Damian turn and hold the door handle, his eyes glued to the thrusts. "We had an urgent, very private matter with our client. We're finishing up. We'll pull out in a second."

A chuckle whips through me.

"You need to leave now." The jingle of keys in the lock makes a point.

Hendrix must have a hell of a lot of trust in Damian. He adjusts his thrusts to keep our skin from slapping as his hot cum streams into me, drips down my legs, and fills the room with his musky scent.

Damian earns my respect. The man on the other side of the door grumbles something.

"We better get you home." Hendrix uses his pocket square to wipe my legs, and Damian repositions his hands, offering his handkerchief before putting both hands back on the door. I notice he's still holding my panties. I've never had someone hold my underwear with such intensity.

"Okay, but I need my panties back."

Damian drags them under his nose before returning them. "You only get them back because I don't want you bare in front of other men."

Hendrix pulls his clothes back on.

I grab the cum-soiled pocket squares and stuff them in my purse. Nothing we can do about the smell.

Three

Damian unlocks the door and steps out first. Hendrix guides me with his hand on the small of my back, keeping me close behind my other boyfriend.

"Now that we're intimately involved with your case, we'll need some time to go over the evidence, then we'll need to meet again." Hendrix confuses me at first, then I catch on that his words are for the three people eagerly waiting for us to clear out of the room.

Once we're in the wide hallway, they walk on either side of me. I follow their lead since we haven't talked about my case yet, but when we end up in the parking garage, I wonder if the fantasy is coming to a close. Some items will remain undone until another time. And I'll probably never do something that crazy again.

"Do we need to set up another meeting to go over my defense?" I say, hopeful that the deal is real.

Hendrix pulls me in by the waist and kisses me like he has something to prove. "You're going home with us."

Damian strokes a hand through my hair and takes my mouth again. His kisses are hungrier than Hendrix's. I want to feed him. I'm lost until the warmth of his lips disappears. "I haven't even gotten started with you. And we don't have to keep up the payment thing. I'd rather just go for broke."

"You were serious? We're really a thing?"

"If we weren't, we wouldn't be allowed to make love to you until your case was over."

"Why not just wait?"

"Because that would be impossible." Hendrix keeps me tight against his hips. His cock is already hard again.

Tangling his fingers in my hair, Damian angles my head to face himself. "When we were walking into the room, Hendrix turned to me and said, 'Get ready to meet our wife.' I had no idea what he meant until I set my eyes on you. Then it all made sense."

"Wife? Wait a minute." The parking garage starts to sway, and Hendrix holds me closer, if that's possible. Damian must realize what's happening because he supports me from behind.

"You feel it, right?" Damian says softly.

"I do."

"Then let's not fight it."

"Can we at least wait until my case is over to get married?"

"Only if you give me a taste of that pussy."

"Have to know if we're compatible, right?" That sounds dorky, but he doesn't seem to mind, based on his erection pressing into my backside.

"Right now." He's dead serious.

I glance over my shoulder, and he motions to a black SUV parked in the corner of the garage.

"Right now...in the car?"

"You think I could taste you on his fingers then watch you orgasm with his dick in you, and not lose my mind when I got cock-blocked?"

"I am ahead of the game on orgasms. What's that you said about going for broke?"

He scoops me up, carries me to the car, and nods to the back. Hendrix opens the hatch and pushes a button that makes the back seat fold down. Damian sets me inside.

"Get your panties off. This is going to be a tight fit."

Us in the back of the car? His *P* in my *V*? All of the above?

He unfastens his pants and drops them to midthigh before climbing in. And yes, it's going to be a tight fit. Hendrix closes the hatch.

Damian guides me onto my back, hovers over me as he kisses my lips, neck, breasts, and works his way down, fitting himself between my legs best he can in the small space. He adds a finger inside of me as he eats my pussy. Is it possible he knows my body better than I do? I've never hit the combo of spots he's finding.

There's no reason to hold back. The faster we finish, the sooner I get some dick, and the less likely someone will catch us. These guys better marry me because I'm ruined.

Hendrix takes a seat in the middle row and turns around to watch. He strokes a finger along the edge of my face. "You're so perfect. I think we were put on this planet to serve you."

I think that's what he says, anyway. Damian has me plowing headlong into my third orgasm of the day. And even though I'd say it's not possible, it's even bigger than the earlier ones. My entire body shakes, and I'm confused by all of the wetness for a second until I realize I squirted on his face.

The embarrassment keeps me from getting too lost in bliss, but I'm the only one who seems to think it's anything other than hot.

"Fuck, love," Damian says. "You trying to drown me?"

"I'm sorry, I never—"

"Don't apologize. Do it every time." Hendrix tucks his finger under my chin and tips my head up.

"I don't know how it happened," I confess.

Damian crawls over me. My scent coats him. "Let's see if you can do it on my dick."

He nudges against my entrance. "You ready for me to make you mine?"

"Yes." I don't understand what it would mean to be his. I don't understand why I'm throwing caution to the wind. I don't understand how we can feel so perfect together. What I do understand is that I can't wait to see how his cock feels.

He uses one slow stroke to seat himself inside of me. I'm so full of cock, I can't think.

"Hendrix was right. Your pussy is perfect. Let me know when you're ready."

Leaning onto one arm as he holds himself over me, he unfastens the buttons in the front of my blouse. My tits spring free. Of all days to be a no-bra day, this was a good one. But I don't want to be free. I want him all over me.

His dick swells inside me. I take another second to adapt.

"Love, you should have warned me your tits were so pretty."

"I didn't know."

"It's hard to believe you're real." Hendrix leans so he can cup one of them, and Damian takes the other with his mouth. My nipples bead, giving the men hard buds to tease.

They're talking crazy, but it feels so good. No need to bring up how normal I am. I squirm under their ministrations.

I'm not sure how Hendrix does it, but one of his hands cups my breasts and the other traces my lower lip.

I let my naughty-girl self shine. Or is it my good girl self? Hendrix and Damian don't seem picky. Teasing my tongue over the tip of his finger, I say, "I wish this was your cock."

Damian's mouth pops off my breast and his hips lurch into mine. "Fuck, I'm about to come."

"Make me yours," I say, not sure if he's asking permission.

He pounds me hard. My tits bounce with his rapid thrusts, and Hendrix manages them both with one hand. It's not graceful as we attempt to sync with Damian, but I suck Hendrix's finger into my mouth, tasting myself.

I want to be full of them. Want to completely surrender. And for now, I do. Damian's thrust angles just right to hit that special spot he'd found with his fingers. In seconds, I'm coming all over his cock. So much for his warning. I beat him to it.

Then he shakes, growls, and spills himself inside me. Pump after pump continues to fill me with his release and it trickles down my ass. Waves of my orgasm come out of nowhere. I'm tossed through bliss and ecstasy. And I don't ever want to go home.

Four

We spend the next two weeks getting the car cleaned, going over my case, and having lots of sex, while playing house in Hendrix's luxurious mountain home. There's no distinction of who sleeps where. We're a trio that does everything together. I'm so addicted, I lose track of the days. If I didn't have my bakery to run and a looming trial date, I'd lose track of time completely.

I schedule the bakery to be closed for a few days before and after Christmas, which gives us tons of time to enjoy each other. And since I'm not sure what to buy either of them for a present, I hit them with the old "let's not do gifts" thing.

That's not likely to work, so I wrap myself in tissue paper and let them tear it off me on Christmas morning. It's better than nothing, and I don't feel so bad when they claim that the lifetime supply of ridiculously expensive underwear and bras they buy me isn't a Christmas present but a necessity.

The holiday flies past, and Hendrix is pissed when he isn't able to settle out of court. My trial takes place on New

Year's Eve. Not the greatest way to end the year, but Mister Benedict, aka Prick, who's suing me, won't back down. He's been told that my legal representation changed but doesn't seem to understand who he's up against. He definitely doesn't understand how protective my lawyers are of me.

Which is why I don't tell them I'm pregnant. I'm not sure how crazy they'll get when they know I'm carrying their child. When Hendrix said he was going to put a baby in me that first day, he must have meant it. Fairly true to form for him... He doesn't joke around much.

When our day in court finally comes, Prick is on the stand, and Hendrix is questioning him. "Have you ever received a settlement for your anaphylaxis?"

"I don't have to answer questions about my medical condition. That's protected under the medical privacy laws."

Hendrix comes back to the table, grabs the papers he suspected he might need, then stands next to the podium. He flips through the pages as he lists each of the dates Prick went to court over his anaphylaxis. Turns out this guy is a real piece of work, putting his life on the line to get payoffs from restaurants.

Since Hendrix is a decent guy, he doesn't bring up our suspicion that Prick has a nurse fetish. Unfortunately, Aria, the nurse who was at my bakery and assisted with his epi pen got pulled in to testify. Little does Prick know that Aria hasn't given him a second thought. She only has eyes for her stepbrothers, but I only know that because they live in the same secluded neighborhood as Hendrix, who happens to be wrapping up his point.

"All of those dates should sound familiar, Mister Benedict. Without infringing on your medical rights, I pulled court documents of the claims you made against restaurants." Hendrix has a powerful command in the courtroom. He seems even bigger than normal.

I catch myself leaning toward Damian and pull back, sitting straight in my chair to avoid a public display of affection even though I could use his snuggle right now.

"I can't help it if restaurants are sloppy with food safety. The bigger question ought to be why you and your intern have sex with your client."

My stomach drops so hard I think the baby kicked. It's too early for that, though.

Murmuring comes from everywhere in the courtroom. How does he know?

"You're not the only one who knows how to do research." Benedict sneers at Hendrix then at Damian and me.

Will this ruin everything? Will he shame us? The judge can bring it all crashing down. My mind goes to the worst possibility. I don't want to be a jailbird mom.

Damian whispers, "Hendrix will handle this."

The judge asks, "Is this true?"

"Your Honor, Yvette was my—our—girlfriend before she was our client."

The judge peers down her nose. "When did you take this case?"

Hendrix gives her the exact date. Fear bubbles through me. Not because Prick just announced to the whole courtroom that I'm in a relationship with two guys, and Hendrix acknowledged it, but because the dates won't work. He has to tell the truth.

"And can you be as specific about the date you began a relationship with Miss Solis?"

"Yes, Your Honor." He gives her the same date.

Her eyes narrow. "Don't play games with me, Counselor."

"I would never do that, Your Honor."

"Then how can you claim to have had a relationship first when she became your client on the same day?"

"If you will allow it, Frank Wallace the public defender can vouch for us."

Damian tracks Frank down, and the rest is history. We win. Prick loses. Hendrix demonstrates his phenomenal ability to handle the courtroom. But I'm more interested in the victory celebration Damian promised. I'll give them the baby news to put a cherry on top of this year.

We're the last case of the day, and Damian tells us to wait while everyone else files out.

Hendrix is antsy. "Believe it or not, this is one of my least favorite places to be. Let's go home for the celebration."

"The celebration has to be here." Damian grins wickedly as he takes Hendrix aside. They look at something he pulls from his bag, then they turn to me, simultaneously dropping to their knees. For a second, I think they have Jell-O legs for once, instead of me.

I figure it out pretty quickly though.

They each hold up a ring box, nod at each other, and say, "Yvette, we love you. Will you marry us, right now?"

I think back to my request that we not get married until after the court case. They'd said they didn't want to wait, but a rather satisfying negotiation had bought me time and orgasms.

"I love you both so much. Yes, with sprinkles on top."

"And cream filled," Damian adds.

"I'll cover it with glaze as long as I get to put some of the cream inside too."

We all crack up as the guys take the rings out of their respective boxes and join them. They're made to go together. The rings and the guys. Then they slip the joined ring onto my finger.

I'm about to share my surprise when Damian calls out, "All right, Bill."

What? The side door opens, and a judge enters. The marriage ceremony happens even though I'm pretty sure we can't all legally get married, but all of our names go on the paperwork. We'll see what happens.

"We can handle the rest. You better get on out of here, Bill," Hendrix prompts.

"Don't disrespect the courtroom." Bill shoots us a look of mock worry.

"You know I have nothing but respect for this legal playground."

"It's the playground part I'm worried you'll get sidetracked by. Just clean up after yourselves." Bill lets himself out, pulling the door shut loudly.

We're lost in a kiss for a moment when Hendrix's hand ends up under my skirt. He's caressing my ass for a minute before I realize he's checking for underwear.

Easing his lips away, he says, "Did you come in this courtroom without panties?"

"Not yet." I wink, and it takes them a second to catch onto my play on words.

"We better fix that," Damian says.

Hendrix lifts me onto the edge of the jury box and works my skirt out from under me. Damian walks into the cordoned area and strips my top off from behind. My baby secret can wait a few minutes.

He makes a *tsk*ing sound in my ear. "No bra either, naughty girl. We happen to know that you have no shortage of undergarments. If we'd have known you weren't wearing any, we'd have had to stop the proceedings to make you pay."

"I would have loved to see the look on the judge's face." Hendrix laughs.

"Or everyone in the gallery," I add too lustfully.

"Does our wifey have a few surprises up her sleeve? Would you like that? Getting fucked in front of people?"

"I don't have sleeves." I raise my arms. "But I'm willing to try anything with you guys."

"Good thing." Hendrix unfastens his pants and wastes no time sliding his cock into my pussy. Damian and I kiss over my shoulder while I lean into him, and he massages both of my breasts.

Hendrix pumps slowly, a mischievous grin on his face.

"What are you up to?" I ask.

"You see that camera in the corner?" He nods over his shoulder.

My grin matches his.

"Smile, wifey. Damian arranged it so we can get this on camera."

"Good thing I like being your naughty girl."

"You're a very good, naughty girl." Hendrix kisses me.

And there it is. I finally understand how to be good *and* naughty.

He whispers on my lips, "Maybe we'll end up with video of us knocking you up."

"Sorry, that's not going to happen." I chuckle.

Confusion halts them in their tracks.

Damian says, "I thought you said you're okay with the camera?"

"I am, but somebody already knocked me up."

"What?"

"Why didn't you tell us sooner?"

Their comments come flying at me so fast I can't decipher their words as they both wrap their arms around me, each one claiming that he did it. And after I convince them that it's still safe to have sex, we turn this courtroom into one of Hendrix's favorite places—where we won my case, got engaged, married, and shared our first moment as a family. And despite Judge Bill's wishes, used it as our sexual playground.

But I'm still a good girl at heart, so I make sure the guys clean everything up before we leave. No time like the present to start practicing my new favorite role—being a mom.

Epilogue

Next November

Tugging Daniella's pink knit cap a little lower, Hendrix plants a kiss on our infant's rosy cheeks. I love how his hardened legal persona vanishes when our daughter is in his arms. Damian is also a softy where our daughter is concerned.

And to say these guys are dedicated to Daniella and me is an understatement. Then again, when I recollect how we met, and how quickly our relationship blossomed, I suppose it's not a surprise that their determination is ingrained.

The guys are accompanying me on a leisurely morning stroll down Main Street so I can Christmas shop. I'm a little behind since Daniella consumed my life in a bigger way than I can put into words. Hendrix, Damian, and I have been content to sit at home, oohing and aahing over our tiny bundle. The guys even cut back their workload to spend more time as a family.

And I spent most of my pregnancy turning Sugar D's nut-free bakery over to my cousin, Scarlette.

As we get to the end of Main Street, having found wonderful gifts in the mom-and-pop stores along the way while Hendrix and Damian have been trading off who carries Daniella and who gets the bags, we're at Sugar D's for a planned snack break.

It's nice not to have to get up before the crack of dawn to get the shop rolling. I'd never survive doing that as a new mom, and I have the utmost respect for women who navigate work and parenting.

Scarlette is my age and doesn't have a serious boyfriend so she should be able to handle the shop for a while.

I stop in the entry and read the flyers on the bulletin board. Scarlette had the genius idea to offer locals a place to post their services and events. She has a good mind for business, which along with her being my favorite cousin, helped me trust the store to her.

A flyer for the Christmas Cherry Auction catches my attention. It was a massive success last year and they're asking for volunteers to auction themselves this year. That gives me a fun idea.

I tear a tab containing contact information off the bottom of the flyer.

Hendrix catches my wrist with his free hand that's not busy holding our baby. I feign surprise—my fun idea kicking off spectacularly as it triggers his protective instincts.

"Take that from her, Damian."

"What?" Damian turns back, sees the slip of paper between my fingers, and strips it from me. He furrows his brow as he reads it. "We don't want her to call Roxy?"

"We don't want her to sign up for the Christmas Cherry Auction." Hendrix points to the flyer.

Damian scrapes his teeth over the corner of his bottom lip. "Now, now, Love... I'm sure you heard that last year's auction ended with a few reverse harems. Are you trying to tell us you want a third guy in our relationship? We're not enough?"

"Just wanted to do my part to raise money for a worthy cause. They're hoping to raise forty thousand for the women's shelter this year."

Hendrix nods at the paper. "Fine. Keep her number and I'll send a donation but there's no way in hell I'm letting people bid on you."

Damian pulls his wallet out and sticks the phone number inside.

Little do they know, I have every intention of putting myself on stage, but I'll sort that out later. Right now, I need a donut.

Getting in line with the male customer Scarlette's helping, I notice my cousin is blushing. And flirting. And fumbling. I don't blame her.

From behind this guy, I have an excellent view of slacks that highlight a very muscular butt and thick thighs to match. He's shoved the sleeves of his Henley up to his elbows and has the tattooed forearms to turn the style choice into swoon-worthy apparel.

And his voice...it's richer and darker than the ganache on our Devilish Delight donuts. I catch myself licking my lips.

Damian clears his throat and is staring at me from my immediate left. If Hendrix wasn't cooing at Daniella, he'd probably be smothering me in a kiss, reminding me that I'm spoken for.

I chuckle, lean to Damian's ear, and whisper, "You have nothing to worry about."

"Your drool said otherwise, Love. First the auction, now this. Do you need a reminder of who you belong to?"

I melt a tiny bit every time he calls me Love, but the thought of a reminder sends shivers of excitement through me.

Hendrix must be paying more attention than I realized. His hand slides over my butt cheek. It's different than an ass grab, more exploratory.

"What's gotten into you, Wifey? How dare you ogle another man while not wearing panties."

Damian raises an eyebrow. "She better not ogle men, regardless of her panty situation."

"Shh," I hiss. "I most definitely cannot handle another man. It's just that..." I make a tiny up-and-down motion with my finger. "Well, I'm not dead, plus I think he's flirting with Scarlette."

"Want me to intervene?" Hendrix asks, a protective tone frosting his words.

"No, don't interfere. If this is a thing, my cousin's one lucky girl."

Growls come from both sides of me. My guys like to think I develop a blind spot when other men are near, but even if I was dead, there's so much sizzle between Scarlette and the mystery man my heart would jolt back to life.

"That does it." Hendrix steps behind the counter, snatches up a bag, and drops two of my favorite donuts in. It's taken him no time at all to get used to one-handed maneuvering—the kind you do with baby-holding, not the porn kind.

Damian and I stare in awe. Scarlette offers to help but he shrugs her off.

Amorette, Scarlette's little sister, enters and stops beside us—our moms were set on the 'ette' endings because they felt it made us sound more feminine.

"Why is Hendrix back there?" Amorette asks.

Before I can answer, which is fine because I'm not exactly sure what's going on, Hendrix spins around and returns to us.

To my surprise, he addresses Amorette instead of me or Damian. "Are you busy?"

She glances at the clock on the wall. "I take over for Scarlette in five minutes."

"Can you hold Daniella?"

Amorette's already reaching for the pink bundle. "Sure, what's up?"

"Yvette's having trouble controlling her cravings. Mind if we use the office?"

My eyes pop wide open. Mortification sets in. Is he basically announcing...

He holds up the donut bag. "The new baby thing is tiring, you know, we never share a meal without someone holding the baby or listening to the monitor. We could use a few minutes for a treat."

What's wrong with me that I assumed we were going to have sex?

Amorette agrees, and Scarlette takes a break from her flirting to add that she doesn't have to leave right away if we want to take more than a few minutes.

"Thanks, but this won't take long." Hendrix grabs a bunch of napkins and leads me to my former office. Damian hustles in behind us.

With the door closed and locked, Hendrix flops the bag on the desk and says, "Get undressed."

Oh! My first thought about his intentions wasn't wrong after all.

Damian sets the shopping bags aside and complies without question. I watch the two of them undress, humored at whatever he has planned.

My sex tingles and my nipples bead, prompting me to glance at the pile of napkins. We're going to need them. I love breastfeeding our little one, but aside from Daniella's cries, there's nothing like an orgasm to make my milk come in—and spray out too.

"What are you propo—"

Hendrix pops one of the donuts into my mouth. "Not another word. I don't know what's gotten into you today—wanting to auction yourself and drooling over other guys—but all of your taunting has my dick rock hard."

He grabs the bottom of my t-shirt and strips me. Then my bra. Damian gets rid of my sweatpants.

I savor the donut, moan, then pull it from my face and make a show of licking my sugared lips. The small room reminds me of the day we met, although the circumstances are far better.

Hendrix clears the office supply caddy and a stack of papers from the desk. "I'm pretty sure you were thinking about having all three of your holes filled when you saw the auction flyer. I know the perfect way to do it. I'm going to sit right here. You're going to sit on my cock. And Damian's going to take your ass."

"And my third hole?" I think I'm being cute, toying with them, taking another exaggerated bite of my donut.

As if orchestrated, Henderson sits on the edge of the desk with his thick, erect cock waiting for me. Damian's hands wrap around my waist as he lifts me. The two of them guide me in

301

place with my boobs in Hendrix's face and my bent legs spread over his lap.

The sensation of his cock slowly filling me never gets old. It's better than comfy sweats, a baggy t-shirt, and a latte while snuggled up to read a book. Being filled by either man reminds me how perfect we are for each other. How they'll do anything to protect me. And that I'm loved.

All I have to do is munch on my donut and have as many orgasms as I want.

"Lift her up a second," Damian says.

Hendrix tucks his hands under my thighs and steadies me as I push upward. My walls clench around his cock, the hint of my orgasm winding tighter as his shaft moves through me.

Damian slides his fingers through my wetness and coats his cock. Then he does it again and uses his slicked finger to breach my puckered hole.

I gasp, then breathe as my body welcomes the two of them.

Hendrix eases me back down to fully seat himself again and my world is full. Love. Lust. Donuts. What more could a girl want?

Damian replaces his finger with his cock, gently entering me as he runs his hands over my back.

Both men hold still, making sure I'm ready. And boy am I ever. The double fullness, and possibly a sugar rush, has the tension inside of me building to crazy heights.

Hendrix holds my breasts up and kisses my nipples, adding another level of stimulation. Then he claims them more aggressively. My body's alive, always at its best when Hendrix and Damian are involved.

The suction on my nipples sends electric jolts to my sex. My clit is hyper-sensitive. My internal walls tighten and relax over and over again. And I pop the last bit of the donut into my mouth. I'm in total heaven.

Then Damian sets the other donut in my hand.

"Eat up. We want you happy in every way," he whispers into my ear.

Correction... *Now* I am in total heaven. Slowly rolling my hips, I take a bite.

Henderson licks the sugar from my lips, bites my donut, then returns to my breasts. He bucks his hips, tipping me past the point of no return. My breastmilk unleashes with the release.

It's happened before, but when I see the devilish way he's looking up at me, I realize he's being quite deliberate. A little milk with his donut.

And it's totally hot. The next wave of my orgasm hits even harder, blinding me to his intense, dark brown eyes fluttering shut as he swells inside of me and then finds his own release.

Trying to stay present for the wanton moment, I tip my donut-holding hand backward. Damian takes a bite then comes undone with us as we each try to keep our sweet ecstasy quiet.

And we live happily ever after!

If you'd like a BONUS SCENE with more sexy shenanigans between Yvette, Hendrix, and Damian, sign up for my newsletter.

Visit my website: https://SylvieHaas.com

And true to my initials, SHhhh, I'll let it be our little secret.

More Bundles by Sylvie Haas

Enjoy!

Eggplant Canyon: Books 1-3

Christmas Cherry Auction: 5 Reverse Harem Romances

Sylvie Haas
Freebies

Do you love bonus content?

Sign up for my newsletter and you'll get access to all of my freebies, and I'll keep you up to date on all of my new releases and special offers.

https://SylvieHaas.com

Sylvie Haas obsesses over dirty-talking heroes who fall hard and fast for the woman of their dreams. You'll find heroes, yes plural, in one book because Sylvie has such a hard time making the heroine choose one possessive guy.

On most days, you can find Sylvie with the wind in her hair, her fingers on the keyboard, and her mind in the gutter as she thinks up new places her characters can get frisky.

Sylvie's books will always deliver a happily ever after, and even though they're short, they'll leave you satisfied!

If you haven't signed up for her newsletter yet, there's still room. The more the merrier!

SylvieHaas.com

SYLVIE HAAS

Printed in Great Britain
by Amazon

52557618R00178